HER EX-MA](

Slick Rock 3

Becca Van

MENAGE EVERLASTING

Siren Publishing, Inc.
www.SirenPublishing.com

A SIREN PUBLISHING BOOK
IMPRINT: Ménage Everlasting

HER EX-MARINES
Copyright © 2012 by Becca Van

ISBN-10: 1-61926-929-5
ISBN-13: 978-1-61926-929-3

First Printing: April 2012

Cover design by Les Byerley
All art and logo copyright © 2012 by Siren Publishing, Inc.

Printed in the U.S.A.

PUBLISHER
Siren Publishing, Inc.
www.SirenPublishing.com

DEDICATION

To Diana, Kristen and Lena, for giving me a chance and for all their hard work and expertise.

Also to my daughter, Jessica. Reach for those dreams and don't let anything stand in your way and stop you from achieving them.

HER EX-MARINES

Slick Rock 3

BECCA VAN

Chapter One

Rachel Lamb glanced in her rearview mirror once more, just to assure herself she wasn't being followed. She had been on the run for the last five and a half months, and was so tired she could barely keep her eyes open. She needed a shower, sleep, and some decent food. She saw the sign indicating she was five miles from the country town of Slick Rock, Colorado. She glanced in her mirrors again, indicated, and changed lanes.

Ten minutes later, Rachel pulled into the parking lot of the Slick Rock Motel and entered the reception office. She needed a bed to crash in for at least the next twenty-four hours. She had spent the last week existing on a couple of hours sleep a night, junk food, and adrenaline. She was on the verge of collapse and knew it was only a matter of time before her body shut down on her.

"How may I help you?" asked the young woman behind the counter.

"I'd like to book a room, please. I'll be paying with cash. Is that all right?" Rachel asked.

"Sure, no problem."

Rachel handed the cash over for her room and took the key from the young woman. She exited the door, walked to her car, grabbed her overnight bag, and entered her temporary accommodation. The first thing she did was shower, then crawled into bed and was sound asleep moments later.

Rachel woke feeling more energized than she had for the last week. It was amazing what a good night's sleep did for one's disposition and energy level. She got into her car and drove back down the main street of Slick Rock, looking for a place to eat breakfast. She parked in a parking lot outside the local diner, exited her car, and entered the cafe. She took a seat at the window and ordered a breakfast of bacon, eggs, and toast, as well as a cup of coffee. Once done eating, she left her money with a tip on the table and walked out the door, looking up and down the street. It was still pretty early, so there weren't many people around.

Rachel breathed in the scent of pure, crisp, clean country air. It was so nice to be able to breathe without smog choking her lungs for a change. She didn't really know where she was going and didn't want to have to spend the rest of her life on the run, but she didn't have much of an option at the moment. There was no way she could go back home. She probably wouldn't live through another twelve hours if she did.

Rachel needed to find herself a job, somewhere she would be paid cash in hand, leaving no paper trail behind. She turned on her heel and walked up Main Street, taking notice of what the town had to offer in the way of convenience stores. She crossed the road and walked down the other side of the walkway, looking into shop windows.

Rachel was walking back toward her car when she noticed a help-wanted ad in the far corner of the window of the diner. She moved closer to read the notice.

Help wanted:

Receptionist/administrative assistant needed to work in the local sheriff's office. For inquiries, please call Sheriff Luke Sun-Walker at 555-7986 or head to the sheriff's office.

Rachel felt her heart pounding in her chest and wondered if she could actually walk into the sheriff's office and apply for the position. She stood studying the sign while her brain raced at a rapid pace. Deciding she had nothing to lose and everything to gain, she hurried to her car.

Rachel stared at the sheriff's office building, took a few deep breaths, and let them out slowly. She had to find a way to keep the panic at bay. The last thing she wanted was for the sheriff to be suspicious of her. She exited her car, walked up the steps to the door, took another deep breath, and entered. There was no one in sight of the counter, which Rachel took as a reprieve and turned to exit the building.

"May I help you, ma'am?" a deep, raspy voice asked from behind her.

Rachel jumped and spun around, her heart pounding out a rapid tattoo. She looked at the massive chest covered in a khaki shirt, swallowed convulsively, and looked up, and up and up, until she was looking into dark-green eyes. She opened her mouth to speak then closed it again when no words formed. The man standing before her was tall, really tall, at least six foot four. He had shoulder-length blond hair, massive broad shoulders, and his face was ruggedly handsome with a square, chiseled jaw, tanned skin, and prominent cheekbones. He looked to be around thirty years old, and he seemed to ooze testosterone, making her want to jump his bones. He was masculinity personified.

"Uh, I was inquiring about the help-wanted ad," Rachel replied.

"Sure. Come on through." He held a small gate open for her to enter behind the counter. "I'm one of Slick Rock's local sheriffs, Damon Osborn."

"Rachel, Rachel Lamb," she replied as she took the sheriff's proffered hand. The feel of the sheriff's large hand engulfing her small, pale hand sent tingles of awareness chasing up her spine. She felt her nipples harden and her pussy clench, begging for the emptiness to be filled. She quickly withdrew her hand and moved a few paces away from the sheriff before turning to face him.

He was staring at her as if she were a last meal to a starving man. Rachel swallowed, knowing the sheriff had heard her loud gulp when the corners of his mouth tilted up. He perused her from head to foot, then back again, making Rachel shift uncomfortably from foot to foot. Her eyes rose to meet his, and she wondered if he had felt or seen her nervous apprehension when he wiped all expression from his face.

"Follow me, ma'am," Damon threw over his shoulder, then turned and led the way down the small hallway.

Rachel watched the sheriff ease into a seat behind his desk then indicate with his hand for her to take the chair opposite. She sat down on the edge of the cushion, her purse clutched in her lap, fidgeting with the handles.

"How old are you, Rachel Lamb?" Sheriff Damon Osborn's voice caressed over her, making her want to shiver again.

"I'm twenty-two, Sheriff. I've had experience working as a secretary and know I can do the job," Rachel stated, lifting her chin to the sheriff, waiting for him to refute her claim. She knew she looked a lot younger than her years. She had been told many times and hoped the sheriff wasn't going to ask for proof of age.

* * * *

"Hm. The hours are 8:00 a.m. till 4:00 p.m. Monday to Friday. You may be called to work the occasional Saturday morning, but that rarely happens. If we hire you for the position, you have to work out a three-month probationary period. If all goes well, then you'd need to sign a contract of employment. Of course, we'll need your social security number, bank account number, et cetera. When can you start?" His eyes once again raked over the small woman before him.

She was such a little thing compared to him and his brothers. She couldn't be more than five foot five inches. Her skin was a smooth, creamy white, her hair as black as night and shimmering with blue highlights beneath the artificial light in his office. She had curves in all the right places. He wanted to strip her naked, let his hands roam over her delectable curves, then fuck her until neither of them could walk straight. The most prominent features on the sexy woman before him were her eyes. Her eyes reminded him of a wolf's. They were such a light blue and seemed to pierce him, right to his soul.

"Um, I–I was hoping I could get paid cash. Y–you see, I–I have had trouble with banks before and don't trust them," Rachel said, her eyes sliding away from Damon and to her left.

"Hm, I'd have to ask the most senior sheriff about that. I've only been in this county for a couple of months. Hold on a minute, and I'll go check with Sheriff Luke Sun-Walker," Damon stated, then rose to his feet and left the room, closing the door behind him.

Damon had no idea what the little woman was hiding, but he had picked up on her lie about her trouble with banks. He intended to get his new partner, Luke, to check Rachel Lamb out before he offered her the job. He was going to have to figure out how to keep her occupied until he got the information he wanted from Luke. He tapped on Luke's office door, entering when he heard Luke call him in.

"What's up, Damon?" Luke asked with a frown, still looking at his desk computer.

"I've got a Rachel Lamb in my office applying for the secretarial job, but she wants to be paid cash. If I had to guess, I'd say she's hesitant about handing over her social security and bank account details. I was wondering if you could run a check on her, just to make sure we're not harboring a criminal, if you let me hire her, that is." Damon ran his hand over his face with impatience.

"What's your gut telling you, Damon?" Luke asked, leaning back in his chair.

"My gut is telling me she's not a criminal, but she is on the run from someone or something. My instinct is telling me she doesn't want to leave a paper trail."

"Hm, okay. I've been trying to get these letters typed up, and since I can't type, it's taking me hours. Why not ask Rachel to prove her skills by getting her to type up these letters for me at the front desk? I'll see if I can get a hold of her wallet and driver's license to run a check on her," Luke replied.

"Thanks, boss," Damon said and began to exit Luke's office.

"How many times do I have to tell you I'm not your boss?" Luke asked with a scowl.

Damon didn't bother to answer. He just grinned and left Luke's office, a stack of letters in his hand.

Damon saw Rachel jump when he opened the office door. He figured she must have been daydreaming, as her eyes still had a bit of that faraway, glazed look about them. When he saw her cheeks flame red, he wanted to ask her what she'd been thinking about, but he kept his mouth closed when she lowered her eyes to the floor.

"Are you all right, Rachel?" Damon asked, staring at her flushed cheeks and wondering why she startled so easily.

"Um, yes, thanks. I just didn't hear you coming back, is all."

"Well, as long as you're okay. Luke wants you to type up these letters for him, to show him your secretarial skills. Once you're done, then we can let you know if you have the job or not."

"Okay. Do I use your computer?" Rachel asked, placing her purse on the floor and reaching out for the letters.

"No, you can use one out near reception." Damon watched as Rachel bent down to retrieve her purse, cursing under his breath. "Why don't you leave your purse there? It's not like anyone in here would steal it."

"Um," Rachel said hesitantly then straightened up. "Okay, lead the way, Sheriff."

"Damon."

"What?" Rachel asked as she followed him back down the hallway.

"My name is Damon, not Sheriff. Here you go. This was the

computer the last secretary used. Hopefully all the software is up to date. We don't get much happening around here other than a few drunks on the weekends, the occasional car accident, but things seem to be picking up since the population of the town is growing. More and more city folks are moving out to the country for peace and quiet, and we seem to be getting busier, the more people arrive."

"I can't say I blame them. The country is so much nicer than city life. People tend to be a lot friendlier, and the air is so much cleaner," Rachel said as she started the computer.

"I'll leave you to it. Just give a holler when you're done."

Damon arrived back in his office to see Luke sitting behind his desk, staring at his computer screen. He saw Luke glance his way then back down to the monitor, his jaw clenched tight, his face grim. Instead of telling Damon what'd he'd found, Luke removed himself from Damon's chair so he could see for himself.

"Son of a bitch," Damon hissed from between his teeth when he saw the BOLO, "Be On Look Out," on Rachel's name as a person who might be a witness in a drive-by shooting. He couldn't believe what he was seeing. The more he read, the more the hair on his nape stood on end. There was no way in hell he was letting Rachel run from him. He vowed to himself then and there, he would protect her with his own life. "Why the fuck isn't she in witness protection? What were those assholes in that city thinking? Goddamn it, I can't believe this shit."

"I called a friend of mine in Miami, Matt Livingston. He's a cop, one I would trust with my life. Matt's brother, Josh, is a retired cop. Matt said it was a coincidence that Rachel had hired Josh as a bodyguard for her mom, to keep her safe. Rachel told him everything, even let him listen to the recorded conversations she had with the Police Commissioner, and of course, he passed it on to Matt. Matt has been working day and night trying to find evidence against the Chief of Police, but so far has come up with nothing. He covered his tracks too well. The only way he's going down is by Rachel, and with the threat to her and her mom, she's too scared to testify. I hate the fact that I've just run a check on her. I've probably just alerted half the Miami police force where she is.

"We have to keep her safe. If anyone finds out where she is, she's dead. Hire her on, full pay, cash in hand. I'll bet that little girl has no place else left to run to. She probably has no place to stay either. Don't you have a spare room in that house you and your two brothers bought?" Luke asked, a frown still marring his face.

"Fuck. I can't believe what that little girl must have been through, is still going through. Yeah, we do have a spare room. Do you really think she'd want to share a place with three bachelors?"

"Only one way to find out. Ask her."

Damon heard the slide of the chair wheels rolling over the timber flooring and signaled Luke. Luke quickly replaced Rachel's license in her wallet, then put it back into her purse. Damon nearly smiled when he noticed Luke leaning nonchalantly against the wall just inside the office doorway when Rachel walked in. He was surprised when she didn't seem to notice his colleague at all. Apparently she only had eyes for him. He had to bite his tongue when Luke grinned at him, waggled his eyebrows, and gave him the thumbs-up.

* * * *

Rachel could see the spark of amusement in Damon's eyes and wondered what was so funny. She handed the handwritten then typed letters over to Damon as she eyed him curiously.

"Don't tell me you've finished already."

Rachel screamed, jerking so hard with fright at the deep voice behind her that the finished letters went flying out of her hand to scatter all around her. She placed a hand to her rapidly beating heart, trying to prevent it from jumping through her chest. "Oh my. You scared the shit out of me."

"I'm sorry, ma'am, that wasn't my intention. I'm Sheriff Luke

Sun-Walker. You must be Rachel Lamb. Pleased to meet you." Luke bent down to the floor, picking up the strewn letters. "I can't believe you finished all these letters so quickly. How the hell did you do that?"

"Haven't you ever heard of mail merge, Sheriff?" Rachel asked as she crouched to pick up a few of the letters.

"What?"

"Don't worry about it," Rachel muttered.

"So, when can you start, Rachel? How about tomorrow?" Luke asked as he straightened.

"Well, I really need to find somewhere to live first," Rachel speculated, nibbling on her lower lip.

"Don't you have a room to rent, Damon?"

"Yeah, just haven't gotten around to placing an ad in the local paper yet," Damon replied.

"There you go. Now that you don't have to worry about finding somewhere to live, you can start work right now. Damon can help you move your stuff later." Luke took Rachel's hand in his own and shook it. "Welcome aboard, darlin'. We'll expect you to come to dinner tonight, as well. I have some errands to run and a patrol to make. Just ask Damon if you need anything."

Rachel watched openmouthed as Luke left without a backward glance. She quickly snapped her mouth shut and turned to see Damon giving her the once-over, *again*. She backed out of Damon's office, intent on catching up on the paperwork stacked up on her desk, since she was now employed at the Slick Rock Sheriff's Department. She wondered if she'd done the right thing. The last thing she wanted to do was put anyone else in danger, but just maybe, she was in the safest place she could be for now.

Chapter Two

Damon could see Rachel waiting nervously for him to get out of his car and lead the way into his house. She was biting at her lip again and clutching her purse in a death grip. He knew she had a lot to be scared of and wanted to try and put her at ease. When he hurried up to the front steps, she moved back, allowing him room. He knew she was trying to keep him out of her personal space and could see the nervous apprehension in her eyes. He wanted to take her into his arms and tell her everything would be all right, but knew it was way too soon. "If you'll follow me, baby, I'll show you to your room." Damon led her down the long, timber-floored hall to the door at the end. He opened the door for her and stood back, letting her precede him into the room. He watched her face as she gazed about the bedroom.

"Oh, it's so nice and big. Are you sure this is the room you were going to rent out?" Rachel asked dubiously.

"Oh, I'm sure, Rachel. You have your own bathroom, that way you don't have to share with anyone else."

"But this is the master bedroom, Damon. I can't take that. You should sleep in here and I'll take your room."

"Not gonna happen, so don't waste your breath. Now, let me help you unload your car. Why don't you pull your car up onto the driveway closer to the front door? We'll have all your stuff in here in no time."

"Um, okay. If you're sure?" Rachel asked again, uncertainly.

"No arguments, baby. From now on, this is your room. Come on, let's get your stuff in. We still have to get ready for dinner at Luke's place."

Between the two of them, it took no more than fifteen minutes to get Rachel's car unloaded. Damon couldn't believe how little Rachel had with her. He realized she had obviously skipped her hometown in a hell of a hurry. He knew he was going to have to fill his brothers in on Rachel's situation and advise them to keep it under their hats. The last thing he wanted was for Rachel to disappear again. He knew she would be safe in Slick Rock. He and his two brothers were ex-military, and even though his youngest brother, Sam, was a mechanic, he had also done his fair share as a Special Forces operative. Between him, his brothers, Luke, and Luke's friends, Tom and Billy Eagle, he knew they would have her back.

Damon left Rachel to unpack then shower and change for their night out with his new friends. He waited for his brothers, Tyson and Samson, to make an appearance so he could give them a heads-up before he took off to shower. He knew Sam would shower and change at his mechanic shop before heading home. Tyson had been at his new hotel overseeing things, making sure everything was ready for the Thursday night crowd of ranch hands, locals, and tourists, who were sure to be out and about. Luke heard his brother's vehicle pull up and stepped outside, not wanting Rachel to overhear him while he explained her situation. He just hoped his brothers were as attracted to the sexy little woman as he was. He didn't want to say he thought Rachel was the woman of their dreams until his brothers formed their own opinions of her. They were going to have to be very careful around the skittish woman, even though he knew she had to have a core of strength to have survived as long as she had on her own. He didn't want her to have to worry anymore, and once they knew her a little better and she knew them, he was hoping she would come clean about the trouble she was in.

Damon met Tyson out on the driveway, watching his brother pull his car into the garage, leaving the automatic door open for Sam, who wouldn't be far behind.

"Whose car?" Tyson asked as he walked over to Damon.

"Our new tenant's."

"What? Why the hell have you leased the master bedroom, for God's sakes, Damon? We were supposed to be holding that for the woman we want to share. What the fuck?" Tyson asked with a scowl.

"Wait, I see Sam's car. Let's wait for him so I don't have to repeat everything," Damon replied, shoving his hands into his pants pockets, hiding his clenched fists from his younger brother. Tyson was Damon's twin and younger than he was by five minutes. The only difference between them was Tyson's height—he was an inch taller than Damon—and his eyes, which were hazel, instead of green. Even though the two brothers looked nearly identical, their personalities were like chalk and cheese. They both had intense, arrogant personalities, but more often than not, Tyson was usually more easygoing than Damon. Sam was a couple of years younger than them, a little shorter in stature, but a lot more muscular. His features were similar to his brothers', but he had light-brown hair and brown eyes, which seemed to draw women to him like a puppy. Sam was also the most lighthearted of the brothers, less serious, but when warranted he could be just as intense, if not more demanding, than Damon and Tyson.

"Whose car?" Sam asked.

"Our new tenant's," Damon replied.

"Huh? I thought we were waiting for—"

"Yeah, that's what I thought. It seems this asshole has made the decision for us. How could you, Damon? We were all supposed to vote on a tenant, not just bring one home," Tyson said.

"Wait just a minute…" Damon began.

"Damon, is it all right if I make a pot of coffee?" Rachel called out the front door.

"You don't have to ask, Rachel. Make yourself at home," Damon called back.

"Thanks," Rachel called, closing the front door behind her.

"That's our new tenant?" Tyson asked, licking his lips, his eyes still glued to the front door.

"Exactly," Damon replied, seeing heat in both of his brothers' eyes.

"Where did you find her?" Sam asked, his voice husky with desire.

"She came into the sheriff's office this morning to apply for the secretary's job. She's new to town and had no place to live. In fact, she's in a shitload of trouble. Luke and I did a check on her, when she asked to be paid cash in hand. She's on the run, has been for the last six months. She's nearly crossed the whole of North America and ended up here. She started out in Miami, Florida, worked her way up to New York, and has been traveling from state to state ever since. She has dark smudges under her eyes. I can tell she's exhausted, and who knows when her last decent meal was." Damon ran his fingers through his hair.

"Who's she running from? An ex?" Tyson asked speculatively.

"I wish," Damon replied. "She's running from her last boss. The Chief of Police in Miami."

"Fuck. How can you want to get mixed up in this shit, Damon? We've only just gotten out of the military. I'm sick and tired of fighting. Why the hell are you harboring a criminal?" Tyson asked, and Damon could see his brother's teeth clench, the muscles in his jaw twitching.

"Oh, she's no criminal. She's a witness to murder. Luke has a cop friend in Miami he knows he can trust with his own life. It seems the Chief in Miami took exception to one of his detectives finding out he was involved with a big drug cartel. Rachel was the bastard's secretary. She'd left work for the day, but had obviously forgotten something. She drove back to the station and was just in time to see a drive-by shooting of the detective. She just happened to be in the wrong place at the wrong time." Damon sighed.

"She identified his car?" Sam asked, anger evident in his voice.

"No. Apparently it was a hired car involved in a drive-by. She saw his face."

"Fuck. Why is she on the run? She should have reported in to the Police Commissioner." Tyson growled.

"She did. She even recorded her conversations with the Commissioner."

"So why isn't he doing anything?" Sam asked.

"She didn't realize the Chief of Police and the Commissioner are related. They're brothers-in-law."

"So what? Law is law, as far as I'm concerned," Tyson ground out.

"You and me both, Ty. It seems the Commissioner threatened to kill Rachel's mother if she so much as spouted a word to anyone about what she saw. Then he advised he would kill her as well. He let her leave his office, since he couldn't do anything to her there without incriminating himself, but she's obviously smart. She hired a bodyguard for her mother and sent her on a six-month cruise. She took off the same night and hasn't looked back since."

"Shit. How the hell do you know all this? Where did you get your information from?" Tyson asked.

Damon told his brothers what Luke had learned earlier that day. He was frustrated and worried that he and Luke had inadvertently put Rachel in more danger. He didn't want her to leave. He wanted her to stay with him and his brothers where they could keep her safe. There was no way in hell he was letting anyone near that little woman. Not in his lifetime.

"So are we agreed? Are you attracted to her as much as I am?"

"I don't know yet, Damon. Let us get to know her a bit before we decide," Tyson mumbled.

"Are we agreed on protecting her?" Damon asked.

"Yeah, man, count me in," Sam replied.

"Yeah, me too, but you're gonna owe me big-time," Tyson negotiated.

"What do you want?" Damon asked.

"I get first dibs," Tyson stated, glaring at Damon.

"I didn't think you had decided yet."

"I haven't, but when and if I do, I'm first."

"Done. If and when you decide, don't push her too hard, too fast. She's likely to bolt. It took a lot of guts for her to apply to work for the law again. One wrong move and she'll be off before we even know about it. Now, I'm going to take a shower. Why don't you two go and introduce yourselves to our new tenant?" Damon threw over his shoulder as he opened the front door, heading for the other bathroom.

Chapter Three

Rachel looked up from her seat at the counter in the kitchen, eyeing the large men warily as they walked in and made themselves coffee. She shifted nervously on her seat as she watched them move about the kitchen. She didn't really want to be leasing a room and sharing a house with three bachelors. But since she only had a few hundred dollars left in her wallet and couldn't take the risk of withdrawing cash and leaving a trail, she didn't have much choice.

"Hey, darlin', I'm Sam, Damon's youngest brother. I'm pleased to meet you, Rachel," Sam stated, holding his hand out in greeting.

"Pleased to meet you, Sam."

"I'm Tyson, Damon's twin and younger by five minutes. Nice to meet you, sugar," Tyson greeted, also holding a hand out for Rachel to shake.

Rachel removed her hand from Tyson's, her eyes going from one brother to the other. They were such rugged, muscular, sexy men. Tyson was nearly the spitting image of Damon, except for his extra height and hazel eyes. Sam was a tad shorter than his older brothers, but more muscular and wider in his chest and arms. She could feel her pussy weeping with desire as she stared at the two gorgeous hunks before her. She had never felt so horny in her life. She'd never wanted to jump any man's bones before, but there was something about these three men that seemed to draw her in. She could feel flames licking up her body as they stood drinking their coffee, staring at her as they leaned on the opposite side of the kitchen counter. She had never felt so vulnerable yet small and feminine in her life.

"So, what do you both do when you're not at home?" Rachel

asked curiously, hoping her voice didn't sound as squeaky to them as it did to her.

"I opened up my own mechanic shop in town," Sam replied with a crooked smile.

Rachel couldn't help but smile in return. Sam's sexy mouth tilted up in one corner and had her heart beating rapidly. She slid her eyes away from Sam and over to Tyson.

"I've opened up a new hotel in town. Apparently the local hotel has been around for years and is close to falling down to the ground," Tyson supplied.

"Hm. So do you have music and dancing at your hotel?"

"I plan to. Just haven't gotten around to it yet. The bar has just finished being outfitted, and I've only been open for two weeks. You'll have to come by one night for a visit."

"I might just do that, thanks."

"Shower's free, Ty," Damon called out as he sauntered into the kitchen and poured himself coffee. "Hm, this is the best coffee I've had in years. What did you do to it, baby?"

Rachel felt her heart leap in her chest and her breath hitch at Damon's endearment. Dear God, but he set her blood racing through her body. She hoped he couldn't see her reaction to him and his hot brothers. She felt her nipples harden, and her pussy clenched with excitement. "Nothing special, I just followed the directions on the bag of grounds."

"Shit. You mean we've been drinking coffee too weak and too strong for nothing? Why didn't we know there were instructions on the coffee bag?" Sam asked with a grin.

"Well, even though it's a sexist comment, I'd have to say, men are always too stubborn to ask for directions or read destructions—oh, I mean instructions." Rachel giggled, covering her mouth.

"Oh, you're asking for it, darlin'. You can't say something like that and expect to get away without retaliation," Sam said with his crooked smile.

Rachel watched him warily as he sauntered around the counter, blocking her into her seat. He must have seen her fear and trepidation, because he halted, placing his hands on his hips as he looked down at her.

"Are you ticklish, Rachel?" Sam asked.

"Um, no."

"Knock it off, Sam," Damon growled at his brother.

"What crawled up your ass?" Sam riposted.

"Nothing. Just don't," Damon commanded.

"Sam was only having a bit of fun, Damon. He didn't upset me." Rachel could feel the tension between the two men and wondered if they were always like this.

"I know. I just didn't want him scaring you, baby. You looked a bit wary, is all," Damon said.

"Hey, I'm a big girl, Damon. I can take care of myself. If I didn't like what Sam was doing, I would have told him to back off."

"Okay, I'm ready. Let's head on out to the Double E Ranch for dinner," Tyson stated from the doorway.

"I'm driving," Damon said, grabbing his keys from the hook above the counter.

"Sure, whatever you want, Damon," Sam said facetiously.

"Come on, sugar, you can sit in the back with me," Tyson said, grabbing hold of Rachel's hand and pulling her out the front door with him.

* * * *

Rachel followed Damon, Sam, and Tyson as they got out of the truck. She didn't know why she had been invited to the sheriff's house. She didn't even know the man. The door was opened by a tall, handsome man, and they were all ushered into the large kitchen. The room was full of ranch hands eager for a meal, and Rachel wondered where they were all going to sit. She saw a small woman wander into the kitchen and felt really dowdy dressed in her jeans and shirt. The woman was tiny, with long black hair, violet-blue eyes, and features that reminded Rachel of a pixie. She walked up to Luke, reached up, grabbed his shirt, and pulled his head down to hers. She whispered in his ear, and he had a look of heat and love focused on the small woman at his side. Rachel had to consciously stop herself from fanning her face as she felt heat suffuse her cheeks. She slid her eyes away from the couple, obviously so much in love. Luke moved to the small woman's side, wrapping an arm around her shoulders, then looked up at Rachel.

"Rachel, I'd like you to meet our fiancée, Felicity Wagner, and my best friends, Billy and Tom Eagle," Luke said.

"Pleased to meet you all. I hope I'm not intruding?" Rachel questioned.

"No. Not at all. Why don't you come into the other dining room with me and I'll get you something to drink?" Felicity asked rhetorically, as she had already wrapped an arm around one of Rachel's and was leading her out of the large kitchen and into the dining room. "You know, I'm so glad to have female company for a change. Don't get me wrong, I love my three fiancés, and Nan—our cook—is fantastic, but it will be good to have someone closer to my own age to talk with. What can I get you to drink?"

"Uh, just a soda will be fine," Rachel replied. She could have sworn Felicity had said she had three fiancés, but didn't want to ask in case she upset someone.

Felicity must have seen her look of bewilderment because she burst out laughing as she handed her a glass of soda. "I'm sorry, Rachel. I'm not laughing at you, but if you could see the look on your face..." Felicity giggled again. "Yes, you heard me correctly. I do have three fiancés. I still don't think I have my head around it yet either, but I love those three men more than my life. So, how long have you been in Slick Rock? I don't think I've ever seen you before."

"Uh, I only arrived last night. I decided I liked the look of this small country town, and when I saw the advertisement for a secretary in the window at the diner, I decided to apply for the position. I was hired this morning, and I will be leasing a room with Damon, Tyson, and Sam, until I can find my own place to live."

"They are such nice guys. They haven't been in town that long themselves, but they are so friendly and such hunks. If I wasn't already in love with my three men, I think I would have chased after those three, myself," Felicity said with a wicked grin.

Rachel didn't know what to say, so she just smiled back at Felicity. She was saved from having to try to find something to say when the six men entered the room. There must be something about country living, because all the men were really tall, sexy, and so handsome it was a wonder they didn't have a flock of women hanging around them all the time.

The meal was simple yet delicious. The company was even better. By the end of the evening, Rachel felt as if she had known Felicity her whole life. They just seemed to click. Rachel had watched how attentive Felicity's three fiancés were to her. They filled her plate with food, made sure she had a drink, and if she looked like she wanted something, it was there within easy reach, placed in front of her by one of her three men. Rachel had never seen the likes of it before in her life. She could see the love and affection the three men had for Felicity, as they continuously looked at her with heat in their eyes. By the time dinner was over and coffee was served, Rachel was so exhausted she could barely keep her eyes open. The last six months on the run were finally catching up with her. She was totally and utterly exhausted. She sat sipping her coffee, hoping the caffeine would be enough to give her a little of an energy boost, enough to see her through the rest of the night.

She didn't quite make it. She had no idea when she fell asleep, but the next thing she knew, she was being carried from the car into the house. She yawned, and her heavy-lidded eyes slid open to stare into the eyes of Sam as he carried her into her room.

* * * *

"Shh, it's okay, Rachel. I've got you. You'll be in your own bed in a minute and then you can get a good night's rest," Sam crooned to her quietly. He watched as the small woman in his arms snuggled up against his chest and promptly fell back to sleep. He gently placed her on the bed, removed her shoes, socks, and jeans, as well as her sweater. He thought about removing her T-shirt and bra, then thought he'd better not. He didn't want their little woman embarrassed and uncomfortable around him and his brothers. He paused as that thought popped into his head, then shook his head slightly and bent back to the task of lifting Rachel and placing her beneath the covers. When she was tucked up nice and safe, he left the room in search of his brothers. They needed to talk seriously about the small woman who had just entered their lives. He just hoped his brothers were on the same wavelength that he was on.

Sam found his brothers in the kitchen sipping from mugs of coffee. He walked over to the coffeepot, poured himself a cup, and sat down at the table across from his brothers. He could feel them looking at him, but he ignored them both for a moment as he took the first few sips from his mug, trying to gather his thoughts. He finally looked up at his older brothers to see the expectant looks on their faces. They knew him too well. He hated that they knew what he was going to say or what he was feeling before he had the chance to voice his opinions.

"Spit it out, Sam. I can see the cogs turning in that brain of yours from over here," Damon stated.

"I want her. I want her to be our woman. I think I started falling for her the moment she stuck her head out the front door this afternoon. I don't want her to leave. I think she could be the woman we have been waiting and looking for. Even though she's afraid, I can still see the fire burning underneath that caution and humor, which she uses as a front. She is so sexy, and her eyes… My God, I could drown in those eyes when she looks at me. So, what do you think?" Sam asked with trepidation, looking from Damon to Tyson and back again.

"We're with you on this, little bro, but we are going to have to be patient. She's such a skittish little filly, which she has every right to be. We've also seen the fire in her eyes when she thinks we're not looking. We like her, as well, and apparently Felicity is a really good judge of character. If the way she took to Rachel on their first meeting is any indication, then I would say that, besides being lonely and scared, Rachel is definitely the woman for us," Damon said.

"How the hell are we going to get her to trust us? We need for her to open up with us so we can begin to court our little woman. And God knows what she is gonna think about us wanting to share her between the three of us," Tyson stated with a frown.

"It didn't seem to bother her about Felicity having three men. In fact, I caught her watching the way Tom, Billy, and Luke pandered to Felicity's every need before she even voiced what she wanted. At first she looked confused, but as the night wore on, I could have sworn I saw her looking at Felicity with envy. I think our little baby would love to have the attention of three men," Damon replied with a grin.

"Let's give her a few weeks to settle in and feel comfortable before we start to make a move on her. The last thing we want to do is scare her off and have her running again. We need her to stay here where we can keep an eye on her and protect her. She's had enough to contend with in her life recently. She needs to stop feeling so skittish around us. I think we should touch her as much as possible so she gets used to us, but if she looks too uncomfortable or is about to bolt, then we'll need to back off. What do you two think?" Sam asked his brothers.

"I think it's a great idea. What about you, Damon?"

"I'm in. I think we should start tomorrow."

Sam looked at his brothers with a grin. If the wicked smiles his brothers gave him in return were any indication of the one on his own face, he knew they were all looking forward to wooing their little woman.

Chapter Four

Rachel walked back toward the side door of the office building, cursing herself for forgetting her cell phone. She was halfway back across the parking lot when she heard a screech of tires and then three dull pops. She watched in horror as one of the detectives from her precinct, who had been heading to his car, fell down to the ground. Blood was seeping out of the detective's chest and pooling beneath his body. His eyes were wide open, but she knew he no longer saw anything. His expression was totally blank. She whipped her head around, horrified to see her boss's face as he sped past her in a strange car. Rachel forgot all about her cell phone, turned, and ran. She was in her car and speeding away from the scene in moments. She made it to the Police Commissioner's offices, but didn't remember driving. Her body was shaking so hard it was a wonder she hadn't had a car accident. She surged through the office doors, screaming at the top of her lungs for the officers on the counter to summon the Commissioner and paramedics. Her teeth were chattering, she felt a cold sweat break out over her body, and her throat was feeling sore and raw from screaming and crying.

"Rachel, wake up." The loud voice penetrated her subconscious mind.

Rachel jerked upright, her eyes snapping open, another sob escaping from her mouth. She stared into the faces of three concerned males crowding around her bed. They were each touching her on the arms and legs, trying to calm her fraught nerves as she came out of the horrors she had just relived in her nightmare.

"Are you all right, baby?" Damon asked as he sat down on the side of the bed, taking one of her hands in his.

"Yes. I'm fine, thanks. Sorry," Rachel rasped out.

"You have nothing to be sorry for, sugar," Tyson said as he crawled onto the end of the bed, stroking her thigh through the bedcovers.

"Do you want to talk about your nightmare, darlin'?" Sam asked.

"No! Um, no. I'm good," Rachel replied, averting her eyes from the three men studying her intently. She had just noticed they were all bare-chested, and even though she was still trying to shake the effects her nightmare had left behind, she would have had to be dead not to notice the three sexy, brawny male bodies on display since they had only taken the time to pull their jeans on.

"Do you think you'll be able to get back to sleep, sweetheart?" Damon asked, a frown marring his brow.

"Uh, yeah. Maybe. I don't know," Rachel replied, twisting her fingers together in agitation.

"Why don't you pull on a robe and we'll make you a hot drink? I think some herbal tea would be better than coffee at this time of night. We'll meet you in the kitchen, sugar," Tyson stated as he rose then left the room, his brothers at his heels.

Rachel sat up in bed staring at the empty doorway. What the hell was she going to do? The three men were bound to ask questions. Questions she wasn't sure she should answer. Even though her gut was telling her she could trust these three men with her life, her head was advising her to be cautious. Rachel sighed as she got up and put on her robe and headed for the kitchen. She would decide what she was going to do later, when she had gotten to know the three Osborn brothers better. Until then, she figured playing her cards close to her chest was the safest and wisest thing to do.

Rachel entered the kitchen to find all three of the brothers seated around the large timber dining table. She took a hesitant step forward then stopped as they all turned toward her. She was so nervous she didn't know what to do. She stood in the doorway of the room clutching her hands together.

"Come and take a seat, Rachel. Tyson made you some chamomile tea. That should help settle your nerves down, hopefully enough so you can sleep some more," Damon said.

Rachel walked over to the table and took a seat at the far end, away from where the three brothers were sitting. Apparently, her choice of the furthest chair wasn't lost on the three men watching her because she saw them frown, but was thankful they were too polite to say anything. Rachel picked up the mug of tea, took a sip, grimaced, and set it down again.

"Thanks for the tea, Tyson," Rachel said gratefully, hoping he hadn't seen her expression when she had tasted the tea.

She lifted her head to stare at Tyson when he roared with laughter. The sound coming from deep down in his belly had Rachel's pussy clenching and her clit throbbing. His hazel eyes were sparkling with merriment, and he had dimples next to his lips. Once he finally had his mirth under control and his laugh was down to a chuckle, he looked over to Rachel.

"Well, thank you, sugar, but I know damn well you're struggling not to throw that tea down the sink."

"Sorry, I was trying not to be obvious," Rachel replied with a smile.

"Darlin', your face is so expressive we can nearly read you like a book," Sam stated with a smirk.

Rachel froze. She felt the blood drain from her face, and she feared she would pass out for a moment as her head swam. She wanted to leap up and run, but fear had her frozen to her seat.

"Rachel, look at me," Damon commanded. "You have no need to be afraid of us, baby. We would never hurt you. We would protect you with our lives."

Rachel could see the three Osborn brothers were trying to portray relaxation in their poses. She'd seen Sam take a deep breath and heard him let it out slowly. She knew they were trying to put her at ease and knew she was being ludicrous. She took a deep breath of her own and raised her head to look at the three men.

"I'm not afraid of you," Rachel stated quietly, her gaze never wavering from the three men in front of her.

"It may not be us you're afraid of, darlin', but something is scaring the shit out of you. Do you want to talk about it?" asked Sam.

"I think I would like to get to know you better, before I reveal all the secrets in my closet."

"Fair enough, but just a word of warning, sweetheart. Don't try and run, because there is no place you can run to where we won't be able to find you. We need to know you're safe, Rachel. We feel a connection to you, and I know you feel that connection, too," Damon said, giving Rachel a look so heated she nearly fell off her chair.

Rachel had to rub her thighs together to relieve the ache in her pussy. Not that it did much to relieve her throbbing, dripping pussy, but she'd had to try anyway. She must have squirmed a little in her seat, because the looks the three Osborn brothers were giving her went from heated to downright volcanic in the blink of an eye. Their lascivious grins were all too knowing for her liking. Rachel quickly lowered her eyes, picked up her mug, and took a gulp. She nearly choked on the foul-tasting tea, jumped up from her chair, and was in the kitchen pouring herself a much-needed and better-tasting cup of coffee.

"You won't be able to sleep if you drink that, sugar," Tyson called over to her.

"I won't be able to sleep anymore anyway, so I may as well drink something that doesn't taste like day-old dishwater. Why don't you three go back to bed? There's no point in all of us losing sleep. Besides, I'll just go read for a while. Good night. I'm sorry I woke you."

Rachel could feel the three Osborn brothers watching her and couldn't help the naughty extra sway she put into her hips. She usually wasn't one to tease, but for some reason she couldn't seem to help herself around those three sexy men.

* * * *

Rachel was up and about before any of the men. She was showered and dressed, feeling fresh in slacks and shirt, her hair tied back in a braid. She had a fresh pot of coffee already brewed and had started fixing bacon and eggs before she heard movement down the hall. Wary, she looked up and gave a smile to Sam and Damon as they sauntered into the kitchen, heading straight for the coffee. She looked back toward the door, wondering where Tyson was. Damon must have seen her curiosity.

"Ty will sleep in this morning since he has to be at the hotel until late tonight. So don't worry about breakfast for him, baby. You know you don't have to cook for us all the time. You're leasing a room from us, Rachel. We didn't hire you to be our cook or housekeeper."

"I know, but I like cooking. I haven't had much of a chance to cook recently."

"As much as we don't expect you to cook for us all the time, darlin', feel free to do so whenever you want," Sam stated, and Rachel heard him take a deep sniff then groan loudly. "I can't remember the last time someone cooked me bacon and eggs, darlin'. You're going to spoil us if you keep this up."

"Well, I'm not promising to cook all the time, but I will definitely do my share," Rachel replied with a smile as she served up the food.

They sat around the table in companionable silence, the only sound clinking silverware on plates. Rachel had served herself a portion a quarter of the size of the men, but they still finished before she was done. Since she hadn't been eating regular meals, she was satisfied long before her plate was half-empty. She pushed the remnants of her breakfast aside and picked up her coffee mug, cradling it in her hands, the warmth seeping into her cold, nerveless fingers. She was still not sure if she had done the right thing by getting a job in the Slick Rock Sheriff's Office, but she didn't have much of a choice.

"You don't eat enough, baby," Damon said, eying her half-eaten meal. "You hardly ate anything last night either. You're going to need to keep your strength up to deal with all the office work Luke and I have for you."

"I'm fine. I've eaten enough for me. If I get hungry later, then I'll get something else to eat," Rachel stated then gulped down the last of her coffee.

She stood and began clearing the table, thankful when Sam and Damon rose to help her. They had the kitchen set to rights in no time. Sam surprised her by giving her a kiss on the cheek before heading out to work, throwing a "Thanks for breakfast" over his shoulder. It took her a moment to compose herself, and then she followed Damon out the door and slid into the passenger seat of his sheriff's vehicle. He held the door open for her, and she watched as he rounded the front of the car and got in the driver's side. Considering the size of the town and lack of traffic, Rachel was surprised it took them fifteen minutes before Damon was pulling up in front of the sheriff's office. Rachel was unbuckled and out the door before Damon could get around to her. He met her on the sidewalk, placed a hand at the small of her back, and guided her up the steps. They both reached for the door at the same time. Rachel's hand was enveloped by Damon's over the door handle, and she waited for him to pull away. She looked up at him when he didn't.

"My brothers and I were raised to treat women like ladies," Damon stated, removing his hand from hers. Rachel looked into his eyes again and saw him watching her to see what she would do. She could see the mischievous gleam in his eyes as he watched her pull her hand from the doorknob then glare up at him, crossing her arms beneath her breasts. He didn't say anything to her, just stood there waiting. He gave a chuckle when she sighed and finally moved away from the door, giving him room to hold it open for her. She yelped when he gave her a tap on the ass as she sashayed past him, her spine ramrod straight and her eyes feeling as if they were spitting fire. She squeaked with indignation and surprise, spinning around to face him. She met his eyes and raised one eyebrow questioningly, then waited to see what he would do, if anything. She opened her mouth to speak then closed it again, frowning at him, spun on her heels, and stomped off to her desk.

She couldn't really berate him for what he had done. She was trying to hide her arousal from him with her indignation. She didn't want him to know she was drawn to him and his brothers. She loved the fact he was being familiar with her. She was so attracted to him and his brothers. The more he, Tyson, and Sam touched her, the more she wanted their touch. What she couldn't seem to get her head around was the fact she wanted all three of the men.

Rachel worked diligently through the morning, trying to catch up on the backlog of paperwork left undone after the previous secretary had left. It took her a couple of hours to sort out the paperwork into piles, marking them from top priority right down to the round file holder most people would call the shredder and recycle bin. By the time she had the urgent work over and done with, her shoulders and back were aching from being stuck in front of her computer monitor. She looked up at the clock to see it was going on two o'clock in the afternoon. She was surprised she hadn't seen anything of Damon or Luke.

Rachel stood up, stretching her arms above her head and giving a groan as her vertebrae popped satisfactorily, then lowered her hands. She grabbed her purse, intending to take a walk and get a sandwich. She had her hand on the doorknob when Damon's deep voice called out to her.

"Where do you think you're going?"

"I'm going to lunch. I presume I get to take a lunch break, don't I, Sheriff?" Rachel replied facetiously.

"Don't get sassy with me, baby. Of course you get a lunch break. I would have thought you'd have had it by now," he said, walking toward her.

"I was so busy trying to clean up all that paperwork, I didn't notice the time."

"I'll bet you didn't even take a coffee break, did you?"

"No. Once I have everything in order, I will take regular breaks because I won't have so much to do. But I couldn't leave that mess on my desk any longer. I can hardly see the timber beneath for the piles of paper."

"Luke isn't a slave driver, Rachel, and neither am I. From now on, take your breaks regularly. It's not doing you any good to sit around without moving for hours on end. Where are you going for lunch?"

"I don't know yet. I thought I'd wander up and down the street until I found somewhere."

"Well, since I was heading out for lunch, as well, why don't we go together? The only decent place to eat is the diner or Tyson's hotel. Since we're going to the hotel for dinner, why don't we head over to the diner?"

"Okay." Rachel reached for the door knob, hesitated, and then pulled her hand back.

"Good girl, you remembered," Damon said with a grin, which earned him a grunt from Rachel as she passed through the doorway as he held the door.

* * * *

The diner was still quite crowded, considering the time of day. Rachel hesitated inside the door as eyes peered at her curiously. Damon wrapped an arm around her waist and led her to an empty booth. A waitress appeared almost instantly to take their order. The young woman had eyes only for Damon and could hardly pull them away from him as he introduced the two women.

"Hey, Damon, what will you have?"

"Hey, yourself, Leah. I'll have the special. This is Rachel Lamb.

She's our new secretary and my housemate. Rachel, Leah Harmer," Damon introduced.

"I'm pleased to meet you, Leah. I'll just have a ham-and-cheese sandwich, please."

"Sure. Would you like anything to drink?" Leah asked.

"Water is fine, thanks."

"Coffee, Sheriff?"

"As if you need to ask, darlin'." Damon gave the young woman a grin and a wink. Rachel saw how Leah's face heated with embarrassment and her eyes with desire as she looked at him.

Rachel watched as Leah's smile spread, lighting up her eyes and face as she turned away. "You've made a conquest there, Sheriff."

"Nah, she's just got a little crush. She'll get over it when the right man comes along." Damon shifted in his chair, obviously uncomfortable discussing himself.

"How long have you lived in Slick Rock?" asked Rachel.

"It's been a few months now."

"Where did you live before?"

"Nowhere, everywhere. Tyson, Sam, and I got out of the Marines a little over six months ago. We decided we'd had enough traveling and taking orders from other people. We wanted to settle and put roots down. We started thinking about finding a woman for us, having a family, and we couldn't do that being Marines. Not if we wanted to have a good family life. We didn't want to have to up and leave our family for months on end, not being able to contact them if the situation prevented it. So we all discussed retiring once our time was up and setting ourselves up in a different life, and as the saying goes, the rest is history."

Rachel was blown away that he had just said he and his brother were looking for a woman to share. Her pussy clenched at the thought of being that woman, and her heart rate sped up. She could just imagine in her mind what it would feel like to have three men loving her, their hands and mouths caressing her body. Her nipples elongated and her panties became damp. She quickly pushed those thoughts aside. She didn't know what to say, so she ignored that part of Damon's conversation.

"You were all Marines?"

"Yeah, baby, but we'd had enough. Where did you live before you came here?" Damon asked. Almost instantly, he reached over the table and took her hand in his. "You don't have to answer that if you don't want to. I'm sorry if I've made you uncomfortable."

Rachel eyed Damon, seeing the sincerity in his eyes. She studied him for a moment, and then comprehension dawned. The knowledge was there for her to see in his eyes and the way he withdrew his question without expecting an answer. He knew. He must have done a check on her. Oh God, she had to get out of here. If he'd checked her out, then she would bet her last dollar they were on their way or already here, looking for her. Her breathing escalated, perspiration broke out over her skin, and her heart pounded inside of her chest. She lowered her eyes, removed her hand from his, rose to her feet, and headed to the restrooms.

Rachel leaned against the sink, breathing deeply, trying to get her panic under control. She met her own eyes in the mirror. Her pupils were dilated, and her eyes were haunted. She turned on the faucet, splashed cold water over her face and wrists, then patted herself dry with a paper towel. She stood there in that lonely bathroom staring at the stranger before her. She could see how frightened she looked and knew without a doubt she had to leave. The door to the ladies' room opened, and she turned, bright fluorescent lights gleaming in her eyes, only allowing her to see the tall silhouette of the man standing in the doorway. Rachel stepped back until her back was pressed against the wall, and a shaky hand rose to her mouth to stop her from crying out in fear. Her legs nearly buckled as the man stepped forward beneath the light. His familiar features releasing her from her paralysis, her legs no longer able to hold her up, Rachel slid down the wall to the floor. She cried out as Damon's strong arms caught her before her ass hit the floor. She wanted to rage at him for scaring the shit out of her, but her earlier adrenaline rush had left her too weak, which just made her angrier.

Damon wrapped his arms around her and hauled her up against his big, warm body. Rachel knew he could feel her shaking and wanted to push away from him, to castigate him for frightening her so badly, but she was going to have to wait until her strength returned. She became aware of him running a large hand up and down her back, soothing her and offering comfort as he made nonsensical crooning sounds.

Rachel's fear finally began to abate, and her strength began to return, as did her fury. She stiffened in his arms, drew away from him, and stood up. She took a step back and stared him down.

"How dare you. You have no idea what you've done. I can't believe you investigated me. Oh my God. I have to leave. Please, take me home so I can pack," Rachel demanded in a fierce whisper.

"Rachel, you can't run for the rest of your life. What sort of life are you going to have, running from town to town, state to state? You can never settle down, get married, and have kids. What about your mom? Are you going to be able to send her on cruises with a bodyguard for the rest of her life? That's called existing, baby, not living."

"At least I'll be alive and so will my mother." Rachel felt tears pool in her eyes then spill down over her cheeks.

Damon rose from his crouch and stepped forward again, grasped her hands, and pulled her into his body, holding her tight against him. "We can protect you, baby. Luke already has word out and about for friends to be on the lookout for any strangers coming into town. My brothers and I are trained Marines. Luke is a sheriff, and his friends, Tom and Billy Eagle, are just as tough if not tougher than he is. You won't be safer than you are here, living and working with ex-Marines and the law. Now, come and eat. We'll discuss everything tonight. I promise everything will work out in the end, baby. Trust me."

Chapter Five

Rachel felt like a specimen under a microscope as she sat in the far corner of the booth in the Slick Rock hotel. Sam was on one side and Damon on the other. Luke was having a conversation with Sam, while Damon greeted Tom and Billy Eagle. Rachel sat watching Tyson as he organized his staff. She knew he wanted to get away to have dinner with his brothers and friends because he kept glancing over toward them. Rachel was so tired she could barely keep her eyes open. She was sipping at her Black Russian—Kahlua, vodka, and cola—and knew she should have stuck to good old plain water. After such a frightening and emotionally draining day, the alcohol was going straight to her head. She was barely aware of what was going on around her, and that was dangerous. She would listen to what Damon and the others had to say, but she was still going to have to pack up and leave. The last thing she wanted was for innocent people to get hurt because of her. No. She needed to leave before that could happen. She would never be able to live with her conscience.

Rachel excused herself and headed for the ladies' room. She was thankful she'd only had half of her drink. She studied herself in the mirror over the sink, taking in the dark smudges beneath her eyes and her half-closed eyelids. *Pretty as a picture,* Rachel berated herself. She shrugged her shoulders. What did she care what she looked like? It was not like she was going to be around much longer anyway.

Rachel's sight blurred. The events of that terrifying afternoon were forever embedded in her mind, only to pop up at the most inconvenient times. The first sob was ripped from deep within her chest, bubbling up her throat and out her mouth. She stumbled into a cubicle, closed and locked the door, and practically fell down onto the closed toilet lid. She buried her face in her hands, trying to contain the furor of emotions determined to spew their way up and out. She covered her face in her hands and let go for the first time in six long months. Once the damn walls came tumbling down, no matter how hard she tried, she couldn't build them up again. She sobbed so hard she could have sworn her ribs moved beneath her skin. She tried to keep her noise to a minimum, but in the end, what did it matter if anyone heard her? They were probably all too busy having a good time to worry about a neurotic, weeping woman. She had no idea how long she sat there sobbing, but it was long enough to make her feel ill. Lucky for her, she was in the right place.

* * * *

"Hi, Damon. Where's Rachel?" Felicity asked.

"She went to the restrooms. Do you mind checking up on her for me, Felicity? She's been gone for a long time."

"Sure, be right back."

Damon watched and waited for Felicity to come out of the ladies' bathroom. He didn't like the fear and panic he saw in her eyes when she finally returned to the table. As soon as he saw her worried expression, he was on his feet heading to the ladies' restroom. Felicity turned and walked with him as she spoke to him.

"She's sick, Damon. I heard her crying and then the sound of her being sick. She wouldn't answer me when I asked if she was all right."

"Thanks, Felicity." Damon pushed open the bathroom door, the sound of Felicity's heels clacking behind him.

"Rachel, unlock the door," Damon commanded gently through the closed door, then stood listening for movement from the other side.

"Goddamn it, Rachel, open the fucking door." Damon yelled this time.

"Felicity, go and get Tyson, Sam, and Luke. I'm going to have to break the door down, and I want one of them on hand in case I need some help with her."

"Wait," Felicity commanded, holding up the palm of her hand. Damon watched as she squatted down, got on her hands and knees, and then put her forehead close to the floor to look under the cubicle door. "I can slide in under the door and unlock it. You won't have to break it down. You need to call for a doctor. She's passed out on the floor."

"Fuck," Damon spat as he watched Felicity shimmy and slide her way under the cubicle door. He heard rustling as she maneuvered around, then the sound of the lock being disengaged.

The doors to the ladies' restroom slammed against the opposite wall as Luke, Tom, Billy, Sam, and Tyson tried to push their way in just as Felicity opened the cubicle door to reveal Rachel slumped half on the floor and half over the commode.

"Luke, call the paramedics or the doc," Felicity commanded as she tried to pull Rachel into her arms, and Damon saw the tears of distress running down her cheeks.

Luke walked up to Felicity and lifted her into his arms, then backed away from the cubicle doorway to give Damon room to get to Rachel.

Damon squatted down to his haunches and checked Rachel's pulse and breathing. The sight of her tearstained cheeks and swollen eyes sent a shard of pain piercing his heart. He scooped Rachel up into his arms then followed Tyson to the private back room. Thankfully there was still a sofa up against the wall, where he deposited his precious bundle. He glanced over his shoulder to see Tyson and Sam staring at Rachel, worried expressions on their faces.

Damon saw Felicity come rushing into the room with a new, clean dishrag, damp with warm water. He was appreciative when she knelt down next to Rachel and began to wipe over Rachel's face and mouth. The sight of Rachel's parchment-white skin, perspiration dotting her brow, made his gut churn and knot with concern.

"Well, now. What seems to be the problem?" Doc Foster asked as he entered the room. "I would like to be left alone with my patient once I know what's going on. So who is going to enlighten me?"

"I went into the ladies' room to hear Rachel crying. Not just usual crying, though, Doc. The gut-wrenching sounds she was making nearly had me crying with her. Then Rachel started being sick, and I rushed out of the ladies' room to get Damon. She was passed out when Damon and I got back," Felicity said, taking a deep, hitching breath when she'd finished.

"Don't you worry none, little lady," Doc said, patting Felicity's hand as he took Rachel's pulse. "You know I'll look after her. Now, leave me so I can examine my patient."

"I'm staying, Doc," Damon stated from his position near the foot of the sofa.

"So am I," Tyson ground out.

"Me, too," Sam avowed firmly.

Damon saw Doc take one look at him and his brothers and knew the stubborn look on his face was enough of an indication that he wouldn't be leaving the room. Doc turned his back on him and began to examine Rachel.

Rachel groaned and opened her eyes just as Doc finished examining her. Doc patted her hand as she opened her eyes. "Well, now. I'm glad to see you back with us, little lady. I'm Doc Foster, but most everyone just calls me Doc. How are you feeling?"

"Tired," Rachel replied with a sigh.

"Yes, well, burning the candle at both ends will do that to you. When was the last time you slept a night through?"

"About six months," Rachel answered, shrugging her shoulders.

"And when was the last time you had a decent meal?"

"Last night and this morning," Rachel answered without hesitation.

"Glad to hear it. You need to eat more, as well as more regularly, and you need more sleep and rest. You are on the edge of utter exhaustion, young lady. If you don't start taking it easy, I'm going to put you into the hospital. I want you to take two weeks off with no stress. Why don't you take a vacation?"

Rachel glanced from the doc, over to Damon, and back to the doc. "I may just be taking one long, permanent vacation very soon," Rachel said with a laugh.

The sound of Rachel laughing so hard and then the laughter turning to tears had Damon's gut clenching with anguish. He wanted to find those bastards after her and wipe them from the face of the Earth. Damon noticed movement from the corner of his eye, and he watched Tyson rush forward and scoop Rachel up into his arms then sit back down on the sofa with her in his lap. He pulled her into his chest and held her as she cried quietly into his body. Damon looked at Tyson and Sam and knew his face mirrored the anguish on theirs. Finally, Rachel's shoulders stopped shaking and her body slumped against Tyson's chest as she fell asleep.

"Thanks, Doc. We'll make sure Rachel takes the time she needs to rest. Since we know we can trust you, I think I should fill you in on a few things," Damon said with a sigh, his hand running down his face in frustration.

Damon spoke quietly, telling Doc everything that had happened to Rachel, why she was on the run, why she was so exhausted and in need of people to look out for her. He watched Doc's face go from stoic to downright furious as he glanced back and forth to Rachel and Damon. By the time Damon had finished explaining, the expression on Doc's face was enough to make any warrior sit up and take notice. He watched Doc rise to his feet, pat Rachel on the shoulder, then leave the room without a backward glance.

"What are we going to do?" Sam asked.

"Anything and everything we can. I was thinking while Doc was examining Rachel. Since none of us can take any time off from work, maybe we should call a few of our Marine buddies. See if they've settled in yet, or are still at loose ends. I don't want to let her out of my sight, but I know damn well if I make her come to the office with me every day, she'll only work herself more into the ground. And what do I do when Luke or I, or both of us, get called out of the office? No, we need some help, and I want no one but trained Marines helping to keep our woman safe. Are we agreed?" Damon asked.

"Agreed," confirmed Tyson.

"Go make some calls, Damon, then we need to get Rachel home to bed," Sam stated.

Tyson reluctantly transferred Rachel over to Sam and went back to work, and Damon stepped out of the room and headed to Tyson's office to make his calls.

Chapter Six

Rachel woke feeling as if she had been dragged through a hedge backward. Her whole body was one big aching mass of nerves. Her eyes and cheeks felt swollen, and then she remembered her breakdown in the ladies' room of Tyson's hotel. She didn't remember much after that, but knew she was in danger. She flung the covers of the bed back, embarrassment heating her cheeks when her totally naked body came into view. *Oh God, who undressed me?* She glanced at the clock on the bedside table to see it was already after ten in the morning. She hurried to the bathroom and was back minutes later, showered and dressed. She grabbed her purse and keys then rushed down the hall to the kitchen. She froze in the doorway when she saw Damon sitting at the dining table, drinking coffee and going through some papers.

"How are you feeling, baby?" asked Damon.

"I'm fine. Why didn't you wake me? And why are you still here?"

"I'm working from home today, and you are no longer employed with the sheriff's office until this thing is over." Damon held his palm up to stop her from interrupting when she tried to argue. "You can't rest if you're working, baby. Doc said you needed to rest, and that is exactly what you're going to do."

"I need money to survive, Damon, and you need a secretary. How can I rest when I won't have money to pay you for leasing your room?"

"You're not leasing our room anymore, Rachel. You are our guest. No, don't go arguing with me. Tyson, Sam, and I have already decided. You will be staying here with us until that bastard and his cohorts are in jail. I have called in a few favors from friends. By tonight, there will be two ex-Marines here to act as your bodyguards. We wanted to do it ourselves, but we haven't been here long enough to take any time off."

Rachel felt her eyes fill with tears, but was determined not to let them fall. She had done enough crying last night to last her a lifetime. As much as she didn't want to put anyone else in danger, she had no money and nowhere else to go.

"Damon, I…thank you."

"Aw, honey, you don't need to thank me. I'm just doing my job. Why don't you take a load off and I'll get you some coffee and breakfast."

"Coffee, I would kill for. Breakfast, I don't have the stomach for."

"You will have some toast at least, baby. You heard what the doc said. Plenty of rest and regular meals. How the hell are you going to have the strength to endure this shit if you don't eat properly? Come on and sit down. Drink your coffee while I make your toast. No arguments." Rachel watched Damon move around the kitchen. He poured her coffee and set it on the table in front of her then headed back to the kitchen and made her some toast. She loved the way he moved. His body was like poetry in motion as his muscles moved beneath his clothes. He sat down and nudged the plate of toast toward her until she picked it up and took a bite.

"You're going to need to tell me what happened if I am going to help you, baby. Are you up to talking?"

"Yeah." Rachel took a deep breath and wrapped her hands around her mug, relishing the comfort the warmth gave her. "I had finished working for the day and had even left the office. I was five minutes up the road when I realized I'd left my cell phone at work. So, I turned around and went back. I was halfway across the parking lot. The doors opened and Detective Mark Reeves was just exiting. I heard the squeal of tires on the tarmac in the lot and turned around to see a car speeding toward him. The popping sound didn't register for a while, but the determination I saw on my boss's face in an unfamiliar car and the smoking gun in his hand did. I turned back to the detective to see him lying on the ground. His eyes were wide open, he had three bullet wounds in his chest, and there was a pool of blood forming beneath his body. I didn't stop to think. I ran to my car and drove to the Police Commissioner's offices. I demanded paramedics be sent for Mark, even though I knew it was too late. I don't know what made me do it, but when I was talking to the Commissioner, thankfully, I hit record on my MP3 player. I told him what I had seen, and he didn't say anything for a while. He just stood there staring at me. When he did speak, it was to threaten me and my mom. He told me if I said anything about what I had seen, he would kill me and then go after my mom. It was obvious he was in this shit up to his neck.

"I ran. I went to my mom's, got on her computer, and booked her on a six-month cruise. I hired a bodyguard to go with her, even though my mom doesn't have a clue. Luckily I had left some clothes at my mom's. I grabbed a bag and packed, took my mom to the airport, where I surreptitiously met her bodyguard, cleaned out my bank account from an ATM machine at the bank, and I haven't looked back since. I have been on the run ever since." Rachel finished her recitation, a hitch breaking her voice.

"Come here." Damon held his hand out to her. Rachel put her hand in his, and he tugged her from her seat, pulling her onto his lap. "You've had a time of it, haven't you, baby? I don't want you to worry anymore. We will do everything within our power to keep you alive and safe."

"I don't want anyone getting hurt because of me, Damon. I couldn't stand it if you or your brothers got hurt."

"You let us worry about ourselves, baby. We are trained Marines, not long out of the service. No one is going to get to us, Rach," Damon reiterated. She tilted her head up when he placed a finger beneath her chin. He stared deeply into her eyes, and she didn't pull away when he slowly lowered his head to hers. She just sat staring back at him, and he lowered his mouth the last couple of inches.

* * * *

Damon groaned against Rachel's lips then slid his tongue into the moist recess of her mouth. Her flavor exploded on his tongue, and with the first taste of her, he knew he would never be able to get enough. He moved a hand to the back of her head, cupping her head to his. He slanted his mouth over hers again and again. His tongue probed over her teeth, the roof of her mouth, her cheeks, and back to slide along her tongue once more. The sounds she made, her whimpering in the back of her throat, had his cock pulsing and straining against the seam of his fly. When Rachel slumped against him with acquiescence, he knew he had to pull back. He slowly wound the kiss down until he was sipping at her lips. He raised his head, taking in her passion-glazed eyes, her red, swollen lips, and pink-hued cheeks.

"Wh–why did you do that?" Rachel asked.

"You are such a sexy little thing, Rachel. Surely you've noticed the way me and my brothers look at you? You can't be that ignorant, surely?"

She obviously didn't know what to say, because she pushed away from him and stood to her feet.

"I don't know what you're talking about." She wouldn't look into his eyes. She kept them averted from his. He watched her pick up her mug and plate and knew she was using the mundane task to recompose herself, taking them to the kitchen and placing them in the dishwasher. Once done, she stood staring out the window into the backyard, her arms wrapped around her waist defensively.

Damon walked up behind her and felt her stiffen when he caged her in by placing his hands on the edge of the sink. He breathed against her ear as he spoke quietly and felt her shiver.

"Don't lie to me, baby, but most especially, don't lie to yourself.

You may not want to admit it, but you want us, as much as we want you. We've seen the desire in your eyes when you look at us. You can't hide the heat in your eyes or the reaction of your body. We are trained to observe every little nuance of body language a person makes. I want you to get used to the idea of being with us. Not one or two, but all three of us. You were made for us, baby. You just have to get used to the idea. So I'm letting you know, from now on, we are going to do everything within our power to keep you by our side and get you into our bed," Damon whispered into Rachel's ear. He kissed her on the temple, straightened, and moved back away, giving her room to breathe and move.

* * * *

Rachel waited until she heard the scrape of the chair on the timber floor and the rustle of paper, indicating Damon was once more seated at the table, before she moved. She walked over to the sliding glass doors and exited into the backyard. She wandered around the yard looking at the plants growing, but not really seeing them. She sat down on a bench seat and breathed in the clean, warm spring air. The feel of the sun on her face was something she hadn't taken the time to enjoy for over six months. The scent of roses and jasmine permeated the air, making her delight in being outside for a change. The garden brought her thoughts around to her mother, who loved to garden.

She missed her mother and the conversations they had had on a regular basis, but knew she was better off staying away from her and her home. She was worried about what she was going to do, because her mother would be heading home in three weeks' time after the worldwide cruise she was on ended. Rachel had used the money she had been saving to buy her own house on paying for her mom's cruise, but didn't begrudge the fact her mom was safe. Nothing was more important to Rachel than her mother. Her dad had died when she was just a toddler. She had been so young she couldn't even remember her father. Her mom had not been interested in remarrying, so she had worked day and night just to keep a roof over their heads and food in their bellies. Rachel felt it was now her turn to try and repay her mother for everything she had sacrificed for her. Not that she expected any gratitude, but Rachel felt guilty her mom was being threatened because of her. She would do anything to keep her mother safe. The sound of Damon's voice calling to her pulled her from her reverie. She turned her head toward the doors and saw him beckoning to her.

Chapter Seven

"Rachel, there're some people I'd like you to meet." Damon indicated to the two big men sitting at his dining table.

Rachel hadn't seen them, as her eyes were still trying to adjust from the bright sunshine to the dim light of the interior of the house. She blinked to clear her vision and moved further into the room. The two men were studying her curiously, their eyes roving over her body, but not in a lascivious way.

"Rachel, I'd like you to meet Seamus O'Hara and his brother Connell. They are going to be staying in the room out behind the garage. They are here to protect you when we can't be with you. Guys, this is Rachel Lamb," Damon introduced.

"Nice to meet you," Rachel said courteously.

"Oh no, the pleasure is all ours, honey. We will do everything we can to protect your sexy little body." Seamus flirted outrageously.

"Knock it off, bro. You're gonna get your clock worked over if you're not careful," Connell said to his brother. "Ignore him, darlin', he's an indomitable flirt. He's like this with all the ladies. Pleased to meet you, Rachel. If there is anything you need, don't hesitate to let us know."

"Thanks, but I'm fine. I really should be going to work. I would be as safe there as I would anywhere else, but the sheriff here has other ideas," Rachel said facetiously.

"You would do well to listen to Damon, Rachel. He knows what he's doin'," Connell explained.

"I'm sorry if I sound ungrateful, because I'm not, but I think the best thing for me to do would be to leave. I don't want anyone else getting hurt because of me. Can't you understand that? I couldn't deal with anyone getting hurt or killed because of me," Rachel stated vehemently, tears of frustration and emotion pricking the backs of her eyes. She glared at the three men before her then turned and rushed from the room.

* * * *

"That went well," Seamus stated.

"Shut up, O'Hara," Damon bit out.

"I think this is the time I should take to settle into our room. You coming, Connell?" Seamus asked.

"In a minute. You go ahead," Connell replied. "She's a little firecracker, ain't she? She's also scared shitless and in love with you."

"What? Do you really think so?" Damon asked.

"Oh, yeah, man. She looks at you like she's dying of thirst. She really does want to try and protect you, doesn't she? She's gonna try and bolt at the first opportunity she gets. I'm going to get Seamus to set up a few remote sensors around the place. They'll let us know if she tries to leave or if someone tries to get at her."

"I appreciate you and Seamus coming to help us. It looks like we're gonna need all the help we can get. Rachel's also on the verge of emotional exhaustion. She collapsed at Tyson's hotel last night. We had to get the doc in to examine her. He's put her on complete rest for the next two weeks. Since she's just started working as mine and Luke's secretary, you can imagine how well that went down."

"Yep, like a hole in the head. I'm going to go unpack, then Seamus and I will set up the sensors. What time will Sam and Tyson get back?" Connell asked.

"Ty will be out until the early hours, but Sam should be back by six, unless he has a rush job on. Do you want a hand setting up?" Damon asked.

"No, we've got it, man. Maybe you should try and talk to your woman," Connell suggested, then headed out the door.

Damon scrubbed a hand over his face. He didn't want to push Rachel too hard too fast, but if he and his brothers didn't try to convince her she was meant for them, they were going to lose her before they even got her.

Damon stood in the doorway of Rachel's room, watching her as she lost herself in a book. The cover on the book piqued his interest, and he moved further into the room to study it. He knew the grin that spread across his face must have looked like a cat after eating a bowl full of cream. The image of one female in sexy lingerie with two bare-chested men surrounding her made his cock twitch in his pants and fill with blood. He moved forward and sat down on the edge of the bed. It took every ounce of his control not to burst out into joyous laughter when Rachel jumped skittishly, trying to hide her book, a guilty expression on her face.

"Oh, I didn't hear you," Rachel said breathlessly as she scrabbled to hide her book.

"Uh-uh, baby. Too late, I already saw the book cover," Damon said, leaning over Rachel's body, his arms on either side of her, caging her in. "You know what this means, don't ya, baby? All bets are off. You are going to end up in bed with me and my brothers. We're not holding back anymore, Rachel."

"Just because I read erotic romance about ménages doesn't mean I want to have one."

Damon did chuckle when she tried to speak as haughtily as she could. But it didn't work, and the sight of her cheeks turning bright red as she glared at him had him laughing even harder.

"Now, how can you say that when you've never had one, baby?"

"I…" Rachel began then snapped her mouth closed.

Damon knew she was stumped for words when she glared at him with frustration. She was obviously so flustered she couldn't think straight.

Damon didn't ease into her this time. He took her mouth beneath his and ravaged her. He thrust his tongue between her lips and teeth, groaning as her tongue intuitively slid along his. He eased his big body over and on top of hers, pressing against her whole length. The feel of her breasts cushioned against his chest had his reflexes kicking in, and he thrust his hips into hers. He licked and nibbled at her tongue and lips, moved his body against hers, trying to get closer without crushing her. No matter what he did, he couldn't get enough. He needed to feel her naked skin sliding on his.

Damon moved the palm of his hand beneath the nape of her neck, holding her in place so he could devour her. His free hand moved between their bodies, and he found the buttons to her shirt, undoing them one by one until he reached the last one. He moved the material of her shirt out of his way and soothed his hand onto the soft, silky, warm skin of her belly. The sound of Rachel mewling in the back of her throat made him go from burning to boiling in seconds. He caressed his way up to her chest, resting the palm of his hand beneath her breasts for a moment. When she didn't protest or move to stop him, he moved his hand those few precious inches until he held her breast in the palm of his hand. The feel of her soft flesh giving as he kneaded it made him growl with unrequited desire.

Damon flicked open the front clasp of Rachel's bra and swept his thumb across the tip of her breast. The feel of her areola puckering with desire, her nipple peaking to his touch, was magic to his senses. He flicked and scraped his thumb rapidly, repeatedly, over her turgid nipple until she arched her chest up into him, begging for more. He slowed the kiss down then licked and nibbled his way down the side of her neck, paying particular attention to all the places that made her body respond to him. He licked down between her breasts until he got to her other breast and sucked her neglected nipple into the heat of his mouth, the sounds Rachel made and the feel of her bucking her hips up into him like music to all his senses.

Damon removed his hand from her breast and slid it down over her body until he encountered the button to her slacks. His deft fingers made quick work of the fastenings, and he moved his fingers to the waistband of her panties. When she didn't protest, he slid his fingers beneath the elastic and didn't stop until his whole hand was cupping her pussy. He groaned with excitement and appreciation as her juices seeped out of her cunt, coating his fingers. He slid two fingers beneath the soft, plump lips of her pussy, caressing from top to bottom, gathering the juices dripping from her body. He slid them back up to the top of her slit, found the excited, engorged nub, and massaged her little button with a light circular motion. The sound of Rachel's scream, the feel of her body shuddering under him as she climaxed, made him feel so strong and masculine.

Damon couldn't wait anymore. He had to have her, now. He eased off her, stood beside the bed, and began to strip his clothes from his body. He saw Rachel watching him remove his clothing, knowing if she decided to call a halt, he would stop and walk away, even if it was the last thing he wanted to do. The sight of her disheveled appearance only turned him on even more. He was back on the bed beside her, and she hadn't made a protest. In fact, she had devoured him with her eyes until she got to his cock. He had seen her eyes widen and her face suffuse with color.

* * * *

Rachel had never seen such a large penis in her life. Actually, she'd never seen one in real life at all. Sure, she'd seen pictures, but the sight of Damon's large, bobbing appendage had her stupefied. She couldn't take her eyes off him. She was jolted from her state of shock when Damon reached for her, sat her up, and pulled her shirt, then bra, from her body. He kept eye contact with her as he removed her slacks, panties, and socks. He eased her back until her head was resting on the pillow and lay down beside her once more. He swept his hand up and down her naked length, from thigh to breast and back again.

Rachel was having trouble filling her lungs with air, panting as if she had just run the hundred-meter sprint. She moved her eyes down her body to see Damon's hand envelope one of her breasts. She couldn't stop the moan of pleasure from escaping her mouth or the thrust of her chest as her body instinctively sought more.

Damon used his free hand to tilt her head back, looked deeply into her eyes, and then lowered his mouth to hers. This kiss was different than the last. It was gentle and full of emotion. He teased and coaxed her into responding to his mouth, easing his tongue between her lips and teeth. He gathered her nipple between thumb and finger, pinching the engorged tip gently.

Rachel opened her mouth and suckled on Damon's tongue. She couldn't get enough of his taste, the feel of his naked body sliding along hers. She wanted to push him onto his back and ride his cock until they were both satiated, but since she'd never had sex before, she didn't really know what to do and wasn't confident enough to take the lead.

Damon moved his body until he was covering hers. The sensation of his chest hair tickling and abrading her hard nipples made her sob with pleasure, and she arched her body up into his. She wanted him, no, needed him more than her next breath. He used his muscular thighs to separate hers, slid his fingers along her sex, and then pushed the tip of a finger into her wet sheath. He pumped his finger in and out of her cunt, gaining depth with every forward thrust. He kissed his way down her body, over her belly, until he reached her mound. He slid down more until his shoulders were between her legs, his face inches above her pussy. He exhaled on her clit, making her buck her hips up into his face. He opened his mouth over her pussy and licked her clit with the flat of his tongue.

Rachel screamed as her body convulsed, her pussy muscles clenching and releasing as pleasure consumed her. When the spasms waned, she felt Damon slide his finger nearly all the way out of her body then push back in and suck her clit into his mouth. Rachel screamed again, her body quaking as another orgasm consumed her. When the pleasure subsided, Rachel realized Damon had his finger in her body as far as it could go, and since she had never had sex before, she felt every nuance of that finger. It was the most wonderful sensation, and she couldn't wait for him to thrust his hard cock into her pussy.

Rachel was held by Damon's eyes as he crawled his way back up her body, lowered himself on top of her, and took her mouth once more with his own. She thought she would be turned off, tasting herself on his mouth. She was surprised to find her flavor mixed with his heightened her passion. When she felt the tip of Damon's cock kiss the flesh of her pussy, she arched her hips up, trying to get his flesh to slide into her sheath. Damon eased back until he was looking at her.

"Do you want my cock in your hot little pussy, baby?" His voice was ragged with desire as she watched him roll a condom over his cock.

"Yes. Now. Please, but be careful with me Damon. I've never had sex before."

"Are you kidding me? Oh my God, Rachel. You don't know how much that pleases me. To know that no one has ever made love to you is such a turn-on. I'll make sure I please you, baby. Just lay back and enjoy. Let me do all the work this first time around. I'll try not to hurt you too much. Tell me if it's too painful, all right, Rach?"

"Okay."

Damon eased his cock into Rachel's cunt. The feel of his steel-hot rod separating her virginal flesh was like nothing she'd ever felt before. Literally and figuratively. Her slick flesh burned as it parted, making way for Damon's cock. The head of his cock popped through her tight muscles, and he held still, giving her body time to adjust to the foreign invasion. He pressed forward gently, filling her more than she ever thought possible.

"Are you all right, baby?" Damon panted.

"Yes. Hurry up and move," Rachel demanded.

Damon laughed but continued to hold still. "There's more of me, baby."

"What? How much more?" Rachel asked breathlessly.

"I'm in about halfway. Don't tense up, baby. I promise I'll fit, and I'll make sure you feel nothing but pleasure once I'm through. Okay?"

Rachel was beyond words, so nodded her affirmation. She felt so full she couldn't believe he was only halfway in. The guy was hung like a bull. Rachel whimpered in protestation when Damon began to withdraw.

"Shh, I'm not going anywhere, Rach. Take a deep breath in and let it out slowly. Good girl. Do it again. That's it," Damon crooned with encouragement. Every breath Rachel took released a bit more tension from her muscles, and he slid more easily. She knew he was waiting for her to relax, and she took another deep breath. She felt his thumb on her clit, massaging it as he surged forward until he was balls-deep in her quivering pussy. He held still for her and waited until her internal muscles adjusted and finally relaxed, no longer fighting his intrusion.

Rachel knew she surprised Damon by the look on his face. She wrapped her legs around his ass, her arms around his neck, lifted her head up to his, and practically growled her demand. "Fuck me, now."

* * * *

Damon eased back out of her body then slid forward again. He moved in a slow, smooth rhythm, initiating Rachel into the pleasures of lovemaking. Rachel's fingers were digging into the muscles of his back, trying to urge him to a faster pace. He gritted his teeth, using anything he could to retain control of his libidinous desire, which was in jeopardy of taking over. Then Rachel did something which nearly blew the top of his head off. She used her pelvic muscles and squeezed his dick so hard he nearly lost his wad. His control snapped. He pulled back and thrust back in, his balls slapping against Rachel's ass with the force. He didn't think he would be able to stop now if Rachel asked him. He withdrew again and again, pumping in and out of her body, increasing his speed with every thrust. The sight of Rachel's full breasts jiggling up and down as he powered into her and the sound of her moans had him on the edge way too soon. He didn't know if he was going to be able to hold off much longer.

Movement in Damon's peripheral caught his eye. He turned his head to see Sam was standing off to the side of the room. His brother was watching him take Rachel for the first time. Damon quickly turned back to his lover to see her head thrown back and her eyes closed.

"I'm not gonna last. Help her over, Sam," Damon commanded desperately as he sat up between Rachel's legs. Damon watched Sam move to Rachel's side. His brother slid his hand down Rachel's body, massaging her clit with his fingers, being careful not to touch Damon, and leaned over and took a nipple into his mouth. Rachel screamed long and loud, her cunt pulsing and squeezing Damon's cock until he could no longer hold off. He roared as cum shot up from his balls out the head of his dick to fill the latex between him and Rachel. He slumped down over her, being careful not to crush her, and waited until his legs stopped shaking and he could breathe more evenly. He eased his way out of Rachel's body, slid down beside her on the bed, and pulled her into his body. He had never been so sated or wrecked from sex before. He knew he was done for. And as soon as his brothers had made love to Rachel as well, they were going to be falling just as hard as he had.

Chapter Eight

Rachel lay on the bed, eyes closed, panting for breath, snuggled with Damon. She had read about sex and had tried to imagine what it would be like with a man. She'd given herself plenty of orgasms over the years, but they didn't even come close to the euphoric bliss she had just experienced. Damon placed a kiss on her neck as he snuggled up to her back. She pushed her hips back into Damon's crotch, giving a teasing giggle. She felt the bed dip at her front, but her brain failed to comprehend.

Rachel's eyes flew open. She hadn't even realized Sam was in the room until her passion-hazed brain had finally picked up on the fact there were two bodies on the bed. She tried to scramble off the bed away from Damon's arms and Sam's eyes.

"What are you doing? Get out of my room," Rachel yelled.

"It's a bit late for that, darlin'. I've just watched you having sex with my brother, and I helped to give you an orgasm," Sam said quietly.

"You did n—Oh my God! Oh my God! Shit. Let me up," Rachel threw over her shoulder to Damon, still trying to move. She wanted to slink away in embarrassment, but neither man would let her budge an inch.

"Settle down, baby. You have nothing to be ashamed or embarrassed about. I told you we were all going to end up in bed together," Damon stated.

"Rachel, stop it." Sam took Rachel's wrists in his hands and pinned her arms above her head, Damon anchoring her legs with one of his muscular thighs. "Stop it before you hurt yourself, darlin'. You can't hide what you feel for us, any more than we can from you. Can't you see how much we need you, Rachel?"

"I don't know if I can handle this. I don't know if I even want to do this," Rachel lied, hoping they couldn't see through her.

"Don't you dare lie to me, darlin'. But especially to yourself. If you could see the way your eyes eat all three of us up when we're with you, you wouldn't try and bother spouting that bullshit. We know we've just met, Rachel, but that just doesn't seem to matter. When something is right, shouldn't you reach out and grab hold of it with both hands? Why throw it away before you even try to make it work? You could be letting something precious escape without even realizing it. We would never hurt you, darlin'. Please think about giving us a chance to be with you and show you how it could be with all three of us," Sam said. He leaned down and kissed her gently, reverently, on the lips, then released her arms, stood, and left the room.

Rachel felt Damon move behind her. He slid his leg from off of hers and pulled her up and into his arms so she was sitting on his lap on the side of the bed.

"Sam's right, baby. Please, give us a chance to show you how good it could be with the three of us. We would never, ever hurt you. We are trained to protect you with everything we have in us. We won't let anything happen to you, Rachel." Damon kissed her temple and set her on the bed beside him. He stood up and pulled his clothes on just as Connell called his name.

"Yeah, I'll be right there. Hold your horses," Damon yelled. He turned back to face Rachel. "Think about it, baby," he said, then left the room.

Rachel gathered up her clothes and headed for the shower to freshen up, her mind caught in a circle of tumult as she stewed over Damon's and Sam's words.

* * * *

Sam met Damon, Connell, and Seamus in the kitchen. The grave looks on their faces made his muscles tense in preparation for what was to come. He knew something bad was about to be revealed. And from the looks on the other men's faces, they already knew something he didn't.

"I've found footprints around the front yard. Someone's been staking out your house. They've even managed to pick the lock on the front window," Connell stated.

"Fuck, that's Rachel's bedroom. Oh shit, you were just outside her window?" Damon asked.

"Yeah, man," Seamus replied with a lewd waggle of his eyebrows. "Sounds like things are good on the home front."

"Shut up, Seamus," Sam bit out. "What we do in our own home is none of your business."

"Hey, don't go getting your panties in a knot. I was only teasing. I'm sorry. No harm, no foul. I think you should check out Rachel's room, just to make sure no one's been in there and planted any devices. I also think she shouldn't be sleeping by herself. Maybe you should move her, or one, or maybe all, of you need to be in that room with her. Especially now we know they've found her. We all know how easy it is to slip in and out of a place without being detected."

"I'm on it," Sam threw over his shoulder as he made his way out of the room and down the hall.

Sam entered Rachel's room just as she exited the bathroom. He saw her baulk as she looked at his face and knew she could see his anger.

"Sam?"

"It's all right, darlin'. Why don't you go to the kitchen and help Damon with dinner? I just need to check something out."

"Okay," Rachel replied, but hesitated on the threshold of her room. "Is there anything I can help you with?"

"No, darlin'." Sam came to her, placed a kiss on her forehead, turned her out the door, and swatted her on the fanny.

Sam went over Rachel's room with a fine-tooth comb and found several bugs in her room. One in the bedside lamp, another behind the headboard of the bed, and yet another inside the bedside table drawer. He checked over every inch of her room and bathroom, thankful he had found the three bugs that had been planted. Whoever had set them must have placed them in Rachel's room last night when they were all out at Tyson's hotel. Rage began to build up in him, and he literally had to force it down. He breathed evenly and deeply, trying to get himself under control. The thought of some bastard coming after their woman made him feel sick to his stomach. Once he was sure he was in full control of his ire again, he headed to the kitchen.

"Oh good, your timing couldn't have been better," Rachel said from across the kitchen, where she and Damon were serving up the food.

Once the platters of food were set on the table and everyone had filled their plates and were talking, Sam saw Rachel relax a little more. He could see she was thinking up a storm from the frown marring her pretty face.

"What did you find?" Damon asked, looking at Sam.

Sam didn't reply. He put a hand in his pocket, pulled out the bugs, and placed them on the table. The silence became deafening.

"What are…" Rachel began to ask, but stopped when Damon held up his palm to her.

Sam saw Seamus lean over and pick up the small devices from the table. He watched Seamus get up, head to the kitchen, and begin searching through drawers. Seamus pulled a tenderizing mallet from the drawer and placed the three bugs on a chopping board. Sam winced as Seamus slammed the mallet down on all three devices, smashing them to smithereens.

"Bugs, darlin'," Sam finally replied.

"What? Do you mean listening devices?" Rachel asked. Damon picked up Rachel's hand, which had been resting on the table between them.

"Yeah, baby. Someone planted them in your bedroom."

"Oh my...I have to leave. Can't you see that? They know where I am. You're all in danger," Rachel said, her voice rising with oncoming hysteria.

"Rachel, please calm down. We will do everything we can to keep you safe," Seamus declared from across the table. "Besides, they will now know we are aware they're here and will be more cautious about trying to get to you, but they will slip up. You don't need to worry. We've all been trained for this sort of situation. We're ex-Marines, honey. No one is going to get to you unless they go through us first."

"That's exactly what I'm worried about. Oh God. Have any of you let Tyson know to be on alert? They could try to get to me through him. He's out working and won't be heading home until the early hours of the morning. Maybe we should go and see him?" Rachel asked.

"Settle down, baby. Tyson is always on alert. It's as natural to us as nectar is to bees. We notice everything around us at all times," Damon answered.

"I called him from your bedroom, darlin'. He knows to be more alert than before. Stop worrying about anyone else but yourself. You're the one that needs protecting, not us. Come on, Rachel, stop thinking and eat your dinner. Everything is going to be all right," Sam reiterated.

Chapter Nine

Since Rachel had slept so late that morning, she stayed up sitting on the sofa in the living room, the television playing quietly in the background as she tried to read her erotic novel. She'd read the same paragraph three times in a row without taking in what she was reading. She finally placed the book on the coffee table, giving up the futility of her persistence. Damon and Sam had gone to bed hours earlier to get a good night's sleep in preparation for work tomorrow. A quick glance at the clock amended that thought to "today."

Rachel sat up straight, her whole body on alert, when she heard a noise at the front door. The sound of a key being put into the lock made her body slump with relief again. Tyson was home. She looked over to the entryway as the door swung open, her eyes drawn to the big, brawny man standing in the doorway. She watched Tyson close and lock the door then make his way over to the sofa, sitting down beside her and taking one of her hands in his.

"What are you still doing up, sugar? You should have been in bed hours ago."

"I slept late, and even though my body's tired, I can't get my mind to stop turning in circles."

"Sugar, you can't keep doing this to yourself. You're going to make yourself sick. Why don't I pour us both a glass of wine? Maybe that'll help relax you enough to fall asleep."

"Actually, that sounds good. I can't remember the last time I had a glass of wine. I was too worried about dimming my senses."

"Do you have a preference, sugar?"

"As long as it's white wine, no," Rachel replied, getting to her feet with a helping hand from Tyson.

Rachel followed Tyson into the kitchen, relishing the feel of his skin against hers. She was reluctant to let him go, but in the end had to in order to let him uncork and pour the wine. Once done, he picked up the glasses and led the way back to the living room. He placed the glasses on the coffee table, sat down, and pulled her down beside him. He pulled her up close to him, picked up the glasses, and handed one to her, then placed an arm around her shoulders, keeping her anchored against him.

"Do you want to talk about what's going on inside that head of yours, sugar?" Tyson asked.

"I...I just don't know what to do anymore, Ty. I know I should leave. The last thing I want is for you, your brothers, or your friends to get hurt because of me. I just don't know what I want anymore."

"Does this confusion have anything to do with you and Damon making love?"

Rachel whipped her head around to stare at Tyson then quickly looked away again as she felt heat rising in her cheeks. *How the hell does he know about that?*

"You have nothing to be ashamed of, Rachel, but you need to know there are no secrets between me and my brothers. We tell each other everything, and some things have no need to be voiced—we just know what the other needs or thinks instinctively. Sam told me when he called to let me know to be on alert after finding those bugs in your room. We all want you equally, Rachel. The thought of loving you with my brothers has me so hot, but the last thing I want to do is have you running scared. You think about what we want with you, and then if and when you're ready, you let one of us know. Come on, it's time we were in bed. Grab your glass and I'll meet you in your room. I'm gonna take a quick shower. Then we can go to sleep."

"What do you mean *we*?" Rachel asked warily.

"From now on, you will have one of us sleeping in your bed with you, sugar. That way we know you'll be safe," Tyson stated as he helped Rachel to her feet.

Tyson led Rachel to her bedroom then left to take his shower. By the time he got back, Rachel was safely tucked up in bed, sipping her glass of wine.

Rachel kept her eyes averted as Tyson walked to the other side of the bed, as he was only wearing a pair of form-fitting boxers. He got into the bed and leaned against the pillow, wrapping an arm around her and pulling her up against his side. The feel of naked flesh beneath her cheek as they half sat, half reclined in bed made her body heat up. He smelled so good. The scent of masculine soap and clean man had her gulping her wine nervously.

"Relax, sugar. I don't bite. Well, I won't, not unless you ask me to," Tyson said with a chuckle. He placed a kiss against her temple and sipped his wine.

Rachel began to relax as the alcohol started to work its way through her blood. Her eyes were becoming too heavy to keep open. She felt Tyson remove the glass from her hand, and then he pulled her down beside him until they were lying flat in bed. She heard him turn the lamp off and slid into a light doze, the sound of Tyson's steady heartbeat enough to send her off into a dream.

Hands, mouths, and teeth nibbled and caressed all over her body. She arched her chest up, pushing her nipples into the warm, moist mouths imparting pleasure on her body. She smiled and stretched up again when she heard the masculine chuckles. Then she was moaning as fingers ran up and down the length of her pussy. A light touch to her clitoris and a finger pushing into her tight, wet vagina and she was mewling and panting for breath. She couldn't get enough of the pleasure being bestowed upon her. Large, warm, gentle hands spread her thighs wide, and the finger at the entrance to her cunt pushed into her body until it could go no further. She bucked her hips up when a warm, wet tongue flicked over her protruding clit. God, she was in heaven, and she never wanted her dream to end.

The tongue at the top of her slit worked her into a frenzy of pleasurable sensation. Her whole body felt languid, her muscles lax and heavy. Her muscles tightened, reaching for a climax which was so close and yet still too far away. She arched her hips up and gave a sob of delight as the mouth on her cunt sucked her little nub in between its lips, bracketing it with gentle teeth and laving over the nerves rapidly. She could feel her cream dripping from the hole in her body, down over her ass to the sheet below. The finger embedded in her pussy slid out to sit just inside then glided all the way back in. It slid out again, and another was added, the sensation of friction along her internal walls adding to the barrage. She couldn't get enough. Yet it was too much. Her body tightened even further, gathering up and stretching like the string on a bow. The fingers twisted around and touched a spot inside her she never knew existed. She screamed as her body snapped, flinging her up like the arrow from a bow, hurtling her into orbit. She shook uncontrollably, her cunt clenching and releasing in wave upon wave of ecstasy.

Rachel's eyes flew open. Both bedside lamps were glowing dimly in the predawn light as three sets of male eyes stared at her heatedly. She was totally naked, laid out before the three Osborns like a virginal sacrifice on an altar. Except she was no longer a virgin.

Rachel felt heat creeping into her cheeks, but she didn't turn away this time. She had decided to enjoy her relationship with the three Osborn brothers for however long it lasted. She could be dead tomorrow, and she wasn't going down without experiencing what could be.

Rachel reached up, her fingers threading into Tyson's hair. She tugged and pulled his mouth down to hers, placing her lips against his. The sound of the low growl he emitted at her boldness made her pussy clench, begging for more. She couldn't believe she was going up in flames again. She'd just had one of the best orgasms of her life while still asleep and dreaming. Surely, she should be satiated. Her body had other ideas. She wanted more, and she wanted it now.

Rachel pushed against Tyson until he lay on his back beside her.

She threw a leg over his hips and straddled his body. She brought her mouth back down to his, sliding hers over his full, moist lips. She was grateful when he took over her tentative kiss, thrusting his tongue into her depths. She tasted him as ravenously as he tasted her, her nipples brushing against the hair on his chest as their mouths met, making her pussy weep with need. She aligned her hips with his, rocking and sliding on his length, the tip of his cock massaging her clit.

She growled with frustration when Tyson pulled his mouth from hers, staring into the depths of her soul. He slid his hand down between their bodies, grabbed his cock, and held it up away from his belly.

"I want you to ride me, sugar. Slide onto me, Rachel. Take me into your body. Please, sugar."

Rachel rose up on her knees, aligned her body with Tyson's, and slowly lowered. The feel of his hard, warm, silky-smooth steel rod separating her flesh and making her burn slightly was pure ecstasy. She hadn't gotten a look at his cock, but by the feel of his flesh trying to merge with hers, the man was huge. They both groaned with pleasure as the head of his cock popped through her tight muscles, but what endeared Tyson to Rachel at that moment was the fact he was letting her control things, waiting for her to be ready to take more of his cock into her depths and not pushing in before. Their gazes met and held, and the heat and fire she could see in Tyson's eyes, she knew was mirrored in her own. But there was something more. It was like she could see to the very depths of his soul, and what she saw there made her breath catch in her throat and tears prick behind her eyes. She lowered her mouth to his at the same time she slid over him, taking him deeper inside of her. She moved back up then plunged down again, taking him into the depths of her body, as well as her heart.

Tyson reached up with his hands, brushed her hair back from her face, and slid his hand down her arms, over her breasts, and down to her hips. He held her still, his cock pulsing inside her, her internal muscles answering by gripping him and releasing again. His hand glided back up to her rib cage, and he pulled her down to meld their mouths once more. Rachel fell into his kiss, answering him and following wherever he wished to take her. The feel of a finger against her anus made her squeal in protest, her muscles gathering to move her body into a sitting position and out of reach of that wicked finger. She pulled her mouth away from his and turned her head to look over her shoulder. Sam was behind her, totally naked, his hand fisting his cock as he massaged her ass.

"I won't hurt you, darlin'. Just lay down on Ty and relax," Sam whispered, moving in closer to her, between Tyson's spread thighs. Sam placed the palm of his hand between her shoulder blades, putting gentle yet firm pressure on her upper back. He didn't relent until Rachel did what he wanted. When she was lying supine, impaled on Tyson's cock, her head turned to the opposite side to find Damon beside them, naked, holding his massive cock in hand.

"I want your sexy little mouth on me, baby." Damon's voice was rough with passion. He slid the tip of his cock over her lips and sighed as she opened up to him.

Rachel didn't hesitate. Just seeing Damon's cock in her face made her crave his taste. She opened her mouth and twirled her tongue around the crown of his dick. The taste of his pre-cum exploded on her taste buds, making her want more of his salty, musky flavor. When she had teased him and herself enough, she opened her mouth wide, sucking him between her lips. She hollowed out her cheeks as she sucked him into the depths of her mouth, the sound of Damon's voice offering instruction only making her burn hotter.

"Oh yeah, baby. Good girl. Suck my cock, Rachel. Do you know how sexy you look with my dick in your mouth? Relax your throat, breathe through your nose, and take me down, baby. Oh fuck, yeah. That's so good. Your mouth is heaven, Rach."

"A little cold lubrication, darlin'," Sam stated, breaking into Damon's speech. "Don't tense up, Rachel. Breathe through your nose, and try to relax. God, you're beautiful. You look so damn sexy with my brothers' cocks in your pussy and mouth. I have to get you nice and lubed, darlin'. We are gonna make you feel so good."

Rachel couldn't answer, so she moaned around Damon's cock as he rocked it slowly in and out of her mouth. The feel of Sam's fingers pushing into her ass was so darkly erotic she squirmed on Tyson's cock. The pleasure-pain was enhanced as her clit slid on his hard rod.

"You're doing good, darlin'. I'm gonna give you some more lube, and then I'm gonna get three fingers into your sweet little ass. Push out for me, Rachel," Sam demanded.

Rachel felt Sam push his fingers into her ass, and she was grateful that he talked to her the whole time, trying to keep her relaxed. He pumped, twisted, and scissored his fingers into her dark hole, until her tight muscles accepted the intrusion and finally relaxed.

Rachel felt Sam move up close to her back and cover her with his body. He leaned down next to her ear and blew his moist breath into her ear canal, making her shiver.

"I'm coming in now, darlin'. I want you to try and stay nice and relaxed. You will feel a bit of pinching and burning, but it should not be painful. I want you to stop me if it's too much. Okay, Rachel?" Sam asked.

She gave him a slight nod of her head and then felt his cock kiss against her skin, and he began to push into her ass. It was a tight fit, and she felt a bead of sweat drip onto her back and knew Sam was using his full control, going slow and easy with her. He pushed into her gently yet firmly until his cock popped through the tight ring of muscles of her sphincter. She moaned at the pinch and burn and heard him panting rapidly. She heard her own sobbing breath and sucked harder on Damon's cock as it slid in and out of her mouth. She wiggled her hips slightly to let Sam know she was ready for more. He pushed in, sliding more easily now the tip of his cock was through her tight muscles. She knew she surprised him when she used her hips and pushed back on him. He was now in her ass. He held still, giving her time to get used to him being inside her back entrance.

Rachel growled in frustration at the lack of movement and heard all three of the men bark with laughter. The laughter turned to groans of approval when she tightened her internal muscles and sucked Damon's cock hard. Her silent demands were not lost on the brothers. She felt Tyson and Sam grab a hold of her waist and hips and begin to move.

Rachel moaned with pleasure as Tyson pulled out of her wet pussy until just an inch of him was still inside her. As he pushed in, Sam pulled out of her ass, the head of his cock resting at the entrance of her anus. The two men in her ass and cunt began a slow-moving rhythm of advance and retreat, moving in counterpoint so one of them was always buried balls-deep in her body as she sucked Damon off. They increased their pace in increments, giving her so much pleasure she felt like crying with the exquisite bliss.

Rachel bobbed her head up and down the length of Damon's cock in time with Tyson and Sam rocking in and out of her body. She could feel saliva dribbling down her chin, but didn't care. All that mattered to her was feeling what the three men were doing to her. She squealed around Damon's cock when Tyson gave an extra wiggle of his hips, hitting a sensitive spot deep inside as his pubic bone massaged her clit.

"Do that again, Ty. She liked that so much she clamped down really hard on my cock." Sam panted as he thrust into her ass again.

"Yeah," was all Tyson managed to get out as he pumped back into Rachel's cunt.

Rachel loved the way Sam talked dirty while they were fucking her. Instead of turning her off, his words only seemed to heighten her passion.

"I can feel her muscles fluttering all around and up and down my dick. She's about to explode." Tyson growled.

"Rachel, pull off, baby," Damon said as he tugged on her hair.

Rachel ignored him, just bobbing faster, taking him in to the back of her throat. She swallowed around him so she didn't drown in her own saliva.

"Rachel, pull off if you don't want a mouthful. I'm gonna come," Damon yelled. Rachel upped the ante. She dug her fingers into the muscles of his thighs and swallowed around the top of Damon's cock. The roar he let loose satisfied her to the depth of her bones. She felt so feminine and powerful, Damon's cock swelling and pulsing in her mouth as his cum spewed out and down the back of her throat. She sucked him hard until his cock began to soften, let him slide on her tongue until the crown of his cock was just in her mouth, cleaned him off, and let him pop free.

"Damn, baby," Damon panted, collapsing on the mattress beside her. "Heaven."

Rachel heard Damon's compliments but was too caught up in her own pleasure to reply. The muscles in her womb and pussy had gathered in tighter than a spring, the sound of Tyson's, Sam's, and her own flesh slapping together as they fucked her an aphrodisiac to her ears. She knew she was sobbing and mewling in demand, but could do nothing to stop it.

"Rachel," Tyson yelled, "come with us, sugar."

And just like that, the tension in her body snapped. She yelled loud and long, her legs quivering, her belly jumping and shuddering as her pelvic floor muscles clamped down on the two cocks buried in her body. The feel of those two huge appendages powering through her convulsing muscles as her body flew up to meet the stars, enhancing her pleasure, was the ultimate in ecstasy, and spots formed before her eyes. She was vaguely aware of her two lovers roaring out their own releases with her, their hands tight on her body, holding her in place as they filled her with semen. She slumped back down onto Tyson's chest and drifted off into the land of slumber.

Chapter Ten

Rachel woke to sun streaming through the cracks around the curtain of her bedroom window. She stretched and groaned as muscles never used quite the way they had been hours earlier protested. She glanced at the clock on the bedside table, horrified to find it was almost eleven o'clock. She threw back the bedcovers, gathered some clothes, and headed to the bathroom.

Rachel found Seamus and Connell sitting at the dining room table drinking coffee, reading the local newspaper. She went to the kitchen counter, grabbed the warm pot of coffee, and poured herself a mug of the precious brew.

"Mornin', honey," Seamus said, looking up at her and giving her a wink.

"Morning."

"Hi, Rachel. It's good to see you got a good night's sleep. I thought you'd probably have trouble. How are you feeling today?" asked Connell.

"I'm good, thanks. So, do you guys have any plans for the day? I'm not used to sitting around being idle. I don't think I could stand having to stare at these four walls for the next eight to twelve hours or so." Rachel sat at the table with the two men.

"Seamus and I really liked the look of this town. We're thinking we may settle here once this fiasco is over and done with."

Rachel grimaced but didn't say anything. She was well aware of the fact these two men had put their lives on hold because of her.

"Hey, Rachel. I'm sorry. That didn't come out the way I meant it. None of this is your fault, sweetheart. Look on the bright side. If the boys hadn't called us to help out, we wouldn't have visited for a long time. Who knows where or what we'd be doing? You've made us start making decisions about what we want a lot sooner than we probably would have. Seamus and I are going to take the opportunity you've inadvertently given us and make the most of it. We grew up on a ranch, and seeing the properties for sale has us salivating to get back into an easier life after such violence. We both love the country and are thinking about buying and making a go of our own ranch," Connell said.

"Well, I'm glad I could be some help," Rachel replied laconically and smiled.

"So, do you want to help go through the property section of the paper with us? At least you'll have something to occupy that overactive brain of yours," Seamus said, a crooked grin on his mouth.

"Sure, why not? When we're done, you two can help me in the garden," Rachel replied with a deadpan tone.

"No problem, sweetheart. We just love tending garden," Seamus replied facetiously.

For the rest of the morning, the three of them scoured the properties listed in the newspaper. In the afternoon they spent time weeding and tending to the large gardens. They had all the weeds pulled, trees and bushes trimmed and cut up and in the compost bin. Rachel sat back on her heels and stretched out her tired muscles. The garden looked so neat and tidy. She felt as if she had accomplished a lot with the help of her two babysitters. She stood, brushed herself off, and headed inside to clean up. She had every intention of having a meal prepared for when the men came home. After showering and dressing in clean clothes, she headed to the kitchen to start.

Rachel was rummaging in the fridge looking for the meat she'd placed on the shelf the night before. She couldn't find it. She'd placed the steaks on a plate to defrost. She turned toward the footsteps coming inside and looked over to Connell. She could feel the frown on her face as the skin between her eyebrows puckered.

"What's wrong, Rachel?" asked Connell.

"You or Seamus haven't taken any steak from the fridge, have you?"

"No, why would we..." Connell began. "Seamus, get in here, now."

The sound of anxiety in Connell's voice as he yelled for his brother had the hair on her nape standing on end. Connell moved over to Rachel, pulled her away from the fridge door, and closed it. He brought her up against the side of his body, his free arm whipping up, a gun in his hand.

"What..." Rachel began.

"Shh, now, honey. Let us do our job," Connell said calmly. Pulling Rachel back into the corner of the kitchen, he approached the pantry. He whipped the door open, glanced inside, and all but shoved her in through the door.

"Stay there till I come get you," Connell commanded, closing her inside.

Rachel felt the walls of the pantry closing in on her. Connell hadn't turned the light on, so she couldn't see, but what was worse, she couldn't hear him or Seamus. They obviously had the skills to move around like cats. Her breath and heartbeat were loud to her own ears. She strained to hear beyond the pantry door, but could hear nothing. She had no idea how long she stood in the pantry, her whole body shaking in a cold sweat of fear. She jumped when the door flew open, only to sag against the shelves behind her in relief when Seamus's face registered in her brain.

Seamus reached in and pulled her out of the pantry and into his arms. He held her close, crooning to her softly until her shaking subsided.

"It's all right, honey. No one's here. Sorry we scared you," Seamus said, stroking a hand down over her back.

"If there's no danger, then why the hell did I just have to go through that?" Rachel spat out, her ire beginning to rise now that she was no longer afraid.

"We had to make sure whoever was here was gone. We're just doing our job, Rachel."

"You m–mean some–someone was here?"

"I'm afraid so, honey, but they're long gone."

"Th–they were here while we were out in the backyard?"

"Looks that way," Connell replied as he entered the room.

"Oh God. What are we going to do? I can't take much more of this." Rachel sobbed, burying her face in Seamus's chest.

"Shh, it'll be all right, honey. We'll catch this bastard. I promise," Seamus declared, determination in his voice. "He's going to slip up, and when he does, we're going to be all over him."

"Damon's on his way home. He's bringing Luke with him so they can check things out," Connell said, coming in closer to Rachel, offering her comfort with the touch of his hand on her shoulder.

Rachel lifted her tear-drenched face from Seamus's chest when she heard the squeal of tires on the concrete driveway and clutched at Seamus with another bout of fear.

"It's Damon, honey. He's come to make sure you're all right," Seamus soothed.

Rachel heard the front door slam and a pair of footsteps moving quickly into the house. She turned her head toward the sound. The flash of fear she saw on Damon's face then the relief following had her pulling away from Seamus and throwing herself at Damon. His arms wrapped tightly around her body, pulling her in close to him, holding her as she cried against his chest.

"Ah, baby, it's all right. I'm here now. You're safe," Damon crooned. He bent down, picked Rachel up into his arms, turned, and walked into the living room. He sat down on the sofa, taking her with him, surrounding her with his big, warm, muscular body.

Rachel breathed in his familiar scent, burrowing into his chest. She couldn't get close enough to him. She wanted to burrow beneath his skin, join her body with his, and never leave. Rachel knew she was in trouble, in more ways than one. She was scared shitless not only that she wouldn't survive her stalker, but that she was in love with three men.

What am I going to do? She felt the same for Tyson and Sam. She was in love for the first time, and it couldn't be just one man. No. She had to do things unconventionally. She loved three men, and they were brothers. She'd gotten herself in so deep, in such a short span of time, she didn't know if she could survive without being near them. She knew she should be running. That was the best-case scenario with someone out to kill her. But she didn't want to. She was being selfish for once in her short life. She was going to reach out and grab hold, not willing to let go. She wanted the three Osborn brothers by her side for the rest of her life, and she was going to fight whoever was after her to get and keep what she wanted.

"Rachel," she heard Sam call out, the front door slamming and footsteps sounding then halting.

"Aw, darlin', come here." Sam plucked her out of Damon's arms and into his own. "Are you hurt, Rach?"

"No, Sam. I'm fine. I was just a little shook up," Rachel replied from the safety of his arms, breathing in his masculine scent mixed with grease and oil.

Rachel drew back so she could see Sam and realized he hadn't taken the time to wash up or change out of his overalls. She gave him a smile when she saw grease on one of his cheeks.

"Do you think we overreacted? I mean, all this just for some missing steak from the fridge," Rachel said with a slight smile.

"No, darlin'. Connell called me and said someone had been in the house when you were no more than yards away. I think we should get you to someplace safer," Sam said.

"I agree," Damon replied.

"But, where?" Rachel asked.

"You let us worry about that, baby. We'll figure something out. Why don't you and Sam go clean up in the shower? He's made you all dirty," Damon said, lightly flicking a spot of grease on the tip of her nose.

"Now, that's the best idea I've heard all day," Sam replied, standing up and taking Rachel with him.

Rachel glanced over her shoulder at Damon, giving him a giggle and a smile as Sam carried her from the room. It felt good to laugh again after such a big scare. She was going to enjoy her shower with Sam to its full extent.

Chapter Eleven

Tyson stormed into the kitchen, taking note of all the men sitting around the dining table. He pinned Damon with his eyes, his stance aggressive as he looked at his older brother.

"Where is she?"

"In the shower with Sam. Who's looking after the hotel?" Damon asked.

"I'm lucky I've got such competent staff. I left Joe in charge for the night. He knows he can contact me if needed, but he'll keep things under control. How's our girl taking all this?"

"She's okay. She was a little shaken up, but otherwise she's fine. I think it's time we set a trap for this bastard. I want him out of our lives. I want to be able to concentrate on our woman and not have to worry about someone getting to her," Damon said, and Tyson saw his brother run a hand through his hair in frustration.

"I agree," Luke said. "We need to get this bastard before he gets to her. I've called in a couple of friends of mine. They're on vacation. They work for the government in a team of operatives that doesn't exist on paper. They are like shadows, moving amongst everyday people, blending in without being noticed. No one will ever know they're here."

"When do they get here?" asked Tyson.

"They arrived last night, man. They were just waiting for me to let you know. You won't know who they are, and you're unlikely to see them. They're that good at their jobs," Luke stated.

"Okay, let's get busy," Damon said. Tyson and the rest of the men sat huddled together, plotting and planning out scenarios. Tyson was in agreement with his brothers and friends. They had a killer to draw out and a woman to keep safe.

* * * *

Sam turned on the shower, checked the water temperature, then began stripping Rachel's clothes off. Once he had her naked, he worked to get rid of his own clothes. He pulled her into the stream of warm water, bringing her up against his naked flesh, relishing the slip and slide of wet flesh on wet flesh. He grabbed the shampoo, washed and rinsed his hair, then grabbed the soap. He lathered his hands up then reached over to Rachel. He slid his hands over every inch of her naked skin, paying special attention to all her erogenous zones. By the time he'd finished, his little woman was moaning and wiggling, trying to crawl into him. He guided her under the spray of water, watching as the soap suds slid down her delectable little body.

Sam smiled when Rachel giggled. Picking up the soap, she lathered her hands and went to work on washing him. By the time she reached his crotch, his cock was a throbbing mass of arousal, bobbing up and down with his heartbeat. The feel of her soapy hands enveloping his hard penis was so good he threw his head back and groaned with pleasure. The little vixen sure learned fast. She stroked him from base to tip, her grip tightening as she got to the head of his cock. He couldn't help but thrust his hips forward, sliding his cock through her palm and fingers.

"You keep that up, darlin', and I'm gonna come in seconds."

Rachel didn't reply. She just stared in awe at his cock, pumping her fist faster over his flesh.

"I'm getting close. I'm gonna come, Rach." Sam growled, throwing his head back and yelling in victory.

Rachel didn't let up until Sam covered her hand with his own, withdrawing it from his now-shrinking cock. She squealed when he picked her up, turned her so her back was against the shower wall, and knelt at her feet. He held her pinned against the wall, hooked her legs over his shoulders, supporting her weight with hands on her waist, and buried his head in her cunt.

The first swipe of his tongue along her pussy had Rachel screaming and shuddering as orgasm overtook her. He was astounded she had gone off from his first touch and couldn't wait to send her over again. He loved that he could do that to her.

"That's one, darlin'. I'm not letting up until you have at least two more." Sam shoved his mouth back into her pussy.

He licked, nibbled, and sucked and knew he was taking her up higher and higher with every touch because she bucked and writhed beneath his mouth. He sucked her labial lips into his mouth and licked and flicked his tongue over her sensitive clit, making her sob with pleasure. He moved his arms down and wrapped them around her thighs. He thrust two fingers into her pussy, pumping them in and out of her body, making sure he hit her G-spot every time. He laved on her clit, curled the fingers he had buried in her cunt up, and sent her over the edge. The sound of her scream rang through his ears as her body shook above him, the muscles of her pussy clamping and releasing, her pussy gushing as pleasure consumed the woman above him.

"What…did…you….do?" Rachel stammered out between breaths.

"I'm just loving you, darlin'," Sam replied, looking up into her face. The sight of her pinned to the wall by his arms, her face flushed, her lips full and red, her body still giving an occasional quake, was such a turn-on he felt his cock filling with blood and his balls aching. He had to feel her flesh enfolding him in her tight, wet warmth, and it had to be now.

Sam eased her legs down from his shoulders, holding her steady until she was stable on her feet. He withdrew his arms from around her and eased up from his squatting position until he towered over her. He gripped her waist, lifted her up, and pinned her to the wall once more. He guided one of her thighs around his hips, nodding with satisfaction when her other leg followed, crossing over and clamping herself to his body. He stared into her eyes, his cock aligning with her hole, and thrust. He buried himself into her depths with one powerful surge, groaning as he felt her flesh and muscles separate then close around his hard cock.

"Darlin', you feel like heaven on earth. I love you, Rachel," he said, looking into her eyes.

"Oh, Sam, I love you, too. God, I can't get enough of you. I can't get close enough. I want to crawl right under your skin and never leave," Rachel moaned out.

"You and me both, darlin'. Now hold on tight, you're in for one hell of a ride."

Sam withdrew his cock from Rachel's body, until he was barely inside her. He held her hips tilted up and powered back into her sheath. The sound of his own grunting and Rachel's higher-pitched groans only seemed to heighten his sexual awareness. He slammed his hips against hers again and again, their flesh slapping together, water making sucking sounds as it slid and caught between their bodies, only to continue its journey down to the shower base.

Sam didn't take it easy this time. He was too far gone to regain control over his body. He thrust and pumped, grunting with the force of him slamming his cock into Rachel's cunt. Sam twisted his hips at the end of each thrust, his pubic bone slamming into Rachel's clit, knowing he was enhancing her pleasure as she sobbed every time he did so. The move enhanced his own pleasure, as well, because he could feel her pussy ripple along the length of his cock. He leaned forward, bent his head, and sucked one of her nipples into his mouth. He scraped the edge of his teeth over the distended peak, loving the sound of her mewling in response. He shifted to her other breast, giving it the same treatment, and then he pulled off with an audible pop, lifting his head and claiming her lips with his own.

Sam moaned into Rachel's mouth and caught her moan in return, until Rachel froze on his body. She went totally silent and still, her body taut and trembling, and he knew she was on the precipice of her climactic release. She shoved her hips forward, screaming into his mouth as she clamped down on his cock, gripping him so hard he swore he could see stars. His body shuddered and shook over hers. He devoured her mouth, swallowing her moans, taking them into his keeping, her body quaking beneath him as she milked his balls and took him over the edge with her. When the last throb and shudder played out, he held her close and stood beneath the spray of the tepid water, staring into her eyes until they could no longer stay connected body to body.

Sam lowered Rachel until her feet touched the floor of the shower. He held her steady then, picking up the soap, gave her and himself another quick wash. He reached over and turned the shower off then grabbed a towel. He wrapped it around her cool, naked body then reached for his own towel. Neither of them said another word as they dried off, but he knew he didn't need to. He could see everything he needed in her eyes and let her see the love he felt for her in his own.

* * * *

Rachel and Sam entered the kitchen dining room hand in hand. The men in the room stopped talking, smiled at her, and then went back to their conversation. Rachel released Sam's hand and walked over to the kitchen counter and the empty coffeepot, and made a fresh pot. She wondered if her face was as red as it felt. She wasn't ashamed of her and Sam's lovemaking, but she wasn't used to having sex then having to face other people. She tried to act as nonchalant as possible, but knew her movements gave her away. They were jerky rather than her normal smooth coordination. Warm arms wrapped around her waist from behind, pulling her up against a hard, male body. She turned her head to see if her olfactory senses were working as well as she thought. Yep, Tyson had her wrapped up and against him.

"You and Sam sure sounded like you were having fun, sugar," Tyson whispered against her ear.

"You heard us?" Rachel spun around in his arms. She realized she'd shouted her question and knew without a doubt her face was now the color of beetroot. "Oh my."

"Don't be embarrassed, Rach. Sex is a natural part of life. We all do it, just some more than others," Tyson murmured, a grin on his mouth. He reached down and placed a finger beneath her chin, tilting her face up to his.

Tyson leaned down and kissed her to within an inch of her life. When he was done, he pulled away, a smug look on his face when he released her. He steadied her as she staggered slightly, then turned back to the dining room, leaving her standing in the kitchen staring after him.

"Hey, baby, is that pot of coffee ready yet?" Damon called a minute later.

Rachel picked up the finished pot of coffee and carried it to the dining table. The men practically dove on the pot, each of them filling their mugs, completely ignoring her. Or so it seemed. She grabbed the now-empty pot, pissed at the fact there was no coffee left for her, and stomped her way back over to the kitchen. She went through the same process and had another pot brewing in moments.

"Rach, come over here, baby," Damon called out to her.

Rachel stomped her way back over to the table, wondering what it was the men needed now. Damon grabbed her around the waist and hauled her onto his lap. He picked up his mug of coffee and brought it up to her lips. She gave a grateful sigh as she sipped from Damon's mug, sharing the aromatic brew with him as she cuddled up on his lap.

"So are we agreed?" Luke's voice penetrated into Rachel's love-hazy mind.

"Yeah," echoed around the room as the rest of the men answered.

"Good. The sooner this is over, the better. Luke's friend in Miami is so close to busting things wide open, the head honchos are going to have no place left to turn to," Damon supplied.

"What are you all talking about?" Rachel asked, curiosity getting the better of her.

"We're going to set a trap for this bastard after you, baby. Before the week's over, we should have him and his bosses safe and secure in the slammer," Damon explained.

"Rachel, we're going to spend the next couple of hours going over our plans. Sam's going to order Chinese takeout, so don't worry about food. We need you to listen carefully, and if you don't like what we want you to do, tell us. We'll find another way to get this bastard off your tail. The whole aim is to keep you alive and well, sugar. If you're willing to do what we want, we want you to have things down pat in your mind so you can do them automatically without having to think. If you don't think you're up to it, say so now, sugar," Tyson said.

"I want to do whatever is necessary so I can be free to live a normal life again. Tell me what to do."

Chapter Twelve

Rachel was ready to go to Tyson's hotel before Damon and Sam. She was looking forward to a night out after the day she'd had trying to memorize the plan they had set out as a trap for the next day. She was full of nervous energy and looking forward to getting out of the house. She sat on the living room sofa, her jean-clad legs crossed and one swinging back and forth. She looked up when she heard their steps on the timber floor. God, they were so sexy, with wide shoulders that tapered down to lean hips and muscular thighs.

"Ready to get out of here, baby?" Damon asked, stopping before her and holding a hand out to her.

"Yes. I'm really looking forward to tonight. I'm glad Tyson will have live music and the dance floor has been set up. I hope you boys know how to dance."

"Well, let's just hope what you call dancing and what we call dancing are the same thing, darlin'," Sam said.

"You know what? I don't care, just as long as we all have fun. Let's go," Rachel said as she stood. She kept hold of Damon's hand and slipped her free one into Sam's. Nothing had ever felt so right.

* * * *

Rachel sat down at the table Tyson had saved for them and took a sip of her drink. The word had gotten out about the live entertainment, bringing people out for a night of music and dancing. The place was packed. Rachel sat between Damon and Sam, watching as people strutted their stuff on the dance floor. She and Damon had just spent the last two songs dancing and were in need of a drink to cool down.

"What do you think of the entertainment?" Tyson asked in Rachel's ear so she could hear him.

She turned her head, grinning at him, giving him the thumbs-up, not wanting to have to yell over the noise.

"You look so sexy when you dance, sugar. You nearly had me losing my load as I watched your sexy little ass and hips swaying to the music."

Rachel couldn't help but burst out laughing, spraying soda all over the place, including down the front of her shirt. She grimaced as she pulled her wet shirt away from her breasts, but was still smiling as she turned back to Tyson. He was staring down over her shoulder at her breasts. Her shirt had been white, and now that it was soaked, she knew he was getting an eyeful. She stood up, grabbing a handful of paper napkins and smirking at Tyson as he moved back, allowing her room to move. She reached up, grabbed him by the front of his shirt, and pulled him until his face was down to her level.

"You are so bad," Rachel said into Tyson's ear.

"Yeah, but you love it, don't ya, sugar? Do you want any help in the ladies' room, cleaning up?"

"Tyson, if you followed me into the ladies' restrooms, you would end up with a lot of angry, desperate females pounding on the door to get in. I'll be fine."

"Oh, you're fine, all right, sugar," Tyson stated with a leer and waggle of his eyebrows. "And you're right, now isn't the time or the place. I can't wait until I can get you home. You're not gonna come up for breath until we're done with you, Rach."

"Is that a warning?"

"Nah, sugar. That's a promise." Tyson breathed against her ear, turned around, and went back to serve behind the bar.

Rachel was still smiling when she entered the ladies' restrooms. She dampened the paper napkins and wiped at her blouse. She knew she was going to have to soak her white shirt, but maybe it wouldn't be so bad if she tried to get most of the stain out now. She threw away the napkins and grabbed some paper towels from the dispenser. The door opened, and a tall woman entered and closed herself in a cubicle.

"You know that stain is not going to come out, don't you?" the woman called.

"I know, but I have to try anyway. I'm a bit anal when it comes to my clothes," Rachel called back.

"Yeah, me, too. Except I would just toss it in the trash, then go out and buy another one." The woman opened the cubicle and stepped up to the sink. She eyed Rachel and her stained blouse in the mirror as she washed her hands. "Definitely trash if it was my shirt."

"I think if I soak it long enough the stain will come out," Rachel said, busy looking at where she was rubbing her shirt. The woman moved closer, but Rachel didn't look up again, figuring she was studying the stained shirt.

The feel of a prick in her neck had Rachel raising her head in surprise. The blurring sight of the tall female withdrawing an empty syringe from her neck was too much of a shock to comprehend.

"Sorry, honey. Just doing my job."

Rachel staggered, the effects of the drug working through her system rapidly. She thought her eyes were still open, but she couldn't see anything. The woman had stopped her from falling to the floor, at least. Rachel was vaguely aware of a male voice close by. Then everything went black.

* * * *

Rachel woke up in a strange, dilapidated room. It was pitch black, but her eyes had adjusted enough for her to see. Her head was throbbing and her mouth was dry, making her tongue feel like it was stuck to the roof of her mouth. She tried to stretch her arms and legs, whimpering with fear when she realized she was tied to the bed she was lying on. She lifted her head, only to slump back down, the pain in her head increasing to unbearable proportions. Her ankles and wrists were tied with rope, secured to the metal rails at the foot and head of the bed. She wasn't going anywhere.

Rachel was just drifting off to sleep again, but her whole body went on alert when she heard a door slam. Footsteps followed, then she heard the squeak of hinges as the door to the room opened. She kept her eyes closed and willed her body to relax, breathing evenly and deeply. If she was going to get out of here alive, she was going to have to keep her wits about her. All of her senses were heightened, since she wasn't about to use her eyes. She knew there was a male in her temporary room by the heavy steps on the timber floor. The steps came closer and closer, and she concentrated on keeping her body lax, her breathing even, but it was difficult because she could feel his body heat and could hear him breathing. She tried not to cringe when his body bumped against the side of the bed and knew she had been successful when no movement or sound came from him except for his breathing. The sound of his familiar voice rang through her ears, reverberating in her eardrums.

"Why the fuck did you have to be there that day, Rachel? Why did you have to go back? Did you know what was going on? No, you couldn't have. I've been too careful. If it wasn't for the mob boss breathing down my neck, none of this would have happened. How the hell was I supposed to know my brother-in-law is the head of the drug cartel? I'd get you out of this if I could, but it's down to either you or me, and I'm too much of a coward. I'm sorry, Rachel," her ex-boss said.

The touch of his hand on her shoulder made her feel ill. It took everything within her not to react. He withdrew his hand, and she finally relaxed at the sound of his receding footsteps. She heard the door close and a key turn in the lock. She had to find a way to untie herself and get the hell out of here. If what her boss said was true, she was in deeper shit than she could ever have imagined.

* * * *

"Where the fuck is she?" Sam yelled. Damon knew his brothers were just as scared and frustrated as he was.

"She went to the bathroom, Sam," Tyson replied. "I asked you both to keep an eye out for her. Why the hell didn't one of you move when she didn't come back out?"

"Stop it, both of you. She's gone, and fighting amongst ourselves isn't going to find her," Damon stated quietly, trying to be the calm one in the storm of raging fear for their woman. "Now, get yourselves together and start looking for clues."

"He's right, you know. You can blame each other, but that isn't going to bring her back," an unfamiliar voice bit into the fray.

"Who the fuck, are you?" Sam asked.

Damon turned and saw his brother's aggressive stance as he stared down the stranger.

"Friend of Luke's. I'm Britt Delaney, and my brother, Daniel." Britt indicated the huge man behind him then held his hand out to Sam, then Damon and Tyson. Britt moved aside to allow his brother room to approach.

"You won't need to look too hard to find your woman," Daniel said, his deep, gravelly voice breeching the silence.

"What do you mean by that?" Tyson asked.

"I planted a tracking device on her. All I need is to power up this little beauty," Daniel said, holding up a gadget. Damon looked at the Delaney brothers and then to his own brothers, hope bursting into his heart at the sight of the specialized tracker.

"Then what are you waiting for?" Sam asked.

"We were waiting for you lot to finish blaming each other. We couldn't have gotten a word in edgewise," Daniel said, a smile making the scar running the length of his right cheek stand out.

"Then let's get to it," Damon stated, indicating they all leave the ladies' restrooms.

Damon followed Daniel Delaney out when he turned and left, the sight of his large, bulky body moving with no trouble through the crowd a relief to him and his brothers. The crowd seemed to part, no persuasion necessary from the big man. How the hell they hadn't noticed the two Delaney brothers in Tyson's pub was beyond his comprehension, but he would be forever grateful. Tyson took the lead when they reached the hallway, leading Damon and everyone else into his office. Damon knew it was better to have this discussion in private where they would be able to hear each other as they planned the extraction of their woman.

Chapter Thirteen

Rachel was so cold her bones were aching. She'd lost feeling in her fingers and toes hours ago, and her bladder was protesting as well. She must have eventually fallen asleep, because the sun was just beginning to rise, light peeking around corners and through the cracks of the worn curtains. She was so thirsty. Her lips felt cracked and dry and her whole body ached, but she was still alive. The squeak of the door hinges alerted her to company. She wanted to pretend to still be unconscious, but the call of nature was impossible to ignore. Her bladder was so full she was in pain. Her eyes flew to the door to land on the face of her ex-boss.

"Ah, good, you're awake. I was a bit worried when you didn't wake up in the allotted time. I'm sorry about all of this, Rachel. If I could go back in time and change things I would."

"What are you going to do to me, Frank? You know you can't get away with this."

"Oh, but I already have, sweetheart. I have too many people covering my ass not to succeed. Why did you come back? If you hadn't, we wouldn't even be here."

"I forgot my cell phone."

"Oh, you mean you had no idea what was going on? It was just a coincidence? You were in the wrong place at the wrong time?"

"Yes, that's exactly what happened, Frank. So, why did you kill Mark?"

"He'd just found out the Commissioner was in it up to his neck. Mark came to me with his evidence, and being the loyal brother-in-law that I am, I had to let Joel know he'd been found out. Of course, the only way out was the detective's elimination, and since he worked in our offices and I was the only one aware of what was happening, I was commanded to do the deed."

"God, Frank. What are you going to do? Kill everyone on the force? You know as well as I do, this thing is going to blow wide open. What are you going to do then?"

"I didn't have a choice, Rachel. Joel was threatening to terminate my wife."

"You mean that bastard would actually kill his own sister? Oh God, I'm a dead woman, aren't I, Frank? Is it you who gets to eliminate me, or is it your angelic brother-in-law?"

"Now, now, don't go all sarcastic on me, Rachel. It really doesn't suit you."

Rachel stared at her ex-boss. Her mind was working at fifty miles an hour, grasping hold of escape scenarios and throwing them to the side. If she could only get him to untie her and leave her alone, she may have a chance at escaping and surviving. The only good thing about being abducted was her men were now out of danger. Hopefully they wouldn't be able to find her, keeping them safe and alive.

"Listen, Frank, I need to use the bathroom. Can you untie me so I can take care of nature's call?"

"I suppose there's no harm in it."

Frank moved closer to the bed, working on the rope binding her. He untied her hands first. The pain of moving her arms after being confined in one position for so long was excruciating, but she pushed it to the back of her mind, shaking her numb limbs to get the blood flowing again. She watched as Frank moved to her ankles, keeping her body as loose as possible, waiting for the right moment. What surprised her was Frank didn't even seem to be on alert. Maybe it was the fact she had worked for the man. She felt the binding fall away, tensed her muscles, and kicked out as hard as she could. Her high-heeled boots connected with Frank's face. The sickening noise of bone crunching was satisfying, and Frank dropped to the ground, out cold. Rachel bounded to her feet, staggering slightly on limbs not wanting to cooperate. She listened intently, moving around Frank's unconscious body until she reached the door. She hadn't heard anyone else in the place, but wasn't taking any chances.

Rachel opened the bedroom door, a crack of light letting her see beyond into the decrepit cabin. The room was totally empty of life, as well as furniture, except for one large armchair. The place was an open-style cabin, for which she was thankful. She could see into every nook and cranny. She eased the door open, holding her breath as the rusty hinges squeaked in protest, and bolted. She was out the front door of the cabin and running through the trees surrounding the remote, dilapidated structure.

Rachel had no idea where she was, but didn't care, her only thought getting as far away as possible. She stumbled over tree limbs and rocks, running for her life. Not once did she stop to look back. Tree branches whipped her face and body, but she didn't feel a thing. Adrenaline gave her the energy she needed to keep going. Her breath came out in panted sobs. Her shirt caught on a limb and ripped, but she still kept going. Rachel had no idea how long or how far she had been running and had no intention of stopping.

Rachel stumbled and fell, going down hard, her palms scraping on rocks, her knees connecting with the hard ground. Her right ankle throbbed like a bitch, and she looked down at her feet. The heel of her boot was hanging off, and that was not what she needed to see right now. She reached down and peeled the leather boots from her feet, biting her lip when her right ankle protested with pain. She ignored it. She stood up on her socked feet, pushed the throbbing pain in her ankle to the back of her mind, and ran.

Rachel came to a ravine. She stopped on the edge, peering down the sheer cliff wall. Her eyes tracked along the sides, looking for a place she could descend and get to the river below. The forest was thick with flora, making it difficult for her to plot a safe course. She gave a sigh of relief when she saw a place where the walls had more rocks, less of a sheer drop, and turned, heading in that direction. She had to walk further away from the edge then double back to where she knew it would be easier to traverse and descend. She stopped when she came to the place she thought would be the most appropriate for her descent. She took a few moments to catch her breath, gathering her strength and determination around her. She was going to need everything she had in her to climb down that rock wall. She was going to completely ignore her fear of heights. She had to. Her life depended upon it.

Rachel lay down on her side and eased her legs over the cliff edge. Her stomach dropped down, doing flip-flops as fear tried to rear its ugly head. She took a deep breath, held and then released it. Her hands gripping the dirt and bush, she eased herself lower until her feet connected with a protruding rock. She tested the ledge, first with one foot, letting her whole weight rest on the rock, her hands still digging into the earth and gripping the branch of the bush. When there was no movement beneath her feet, she released one hand and scrabbled for purchase lower down. Slowly, she made her way down to the bottom of the ravine.

Rachel had no idea how much time had passed and didn't really care. She was down on solid ground, her arms and legs weak from exertion and adrenaline from her long, hard descent. She wobbled her way over to the small river, dipping her filthy hands into the cool water, and washed the blood away then cupped her hands and drank deeply. The sun was low to the west of her. She only had a couple of hours before the sun set. Her whole body was aching, every scrape, cut, and abrasion making itself known, and she was so tired she could have lain where she was to sleep the night through. But she couldn't. She needed to find a place to hide. There was no doubt in her mind Frank would be out looking for her. She hoped he hadn't called anyone else in to help.

Rachel stood, crying out in pain as her right ankle and cut feet protested. She wanted to sit back down and soak her aches and pains away in the cold water, but that wasn't an option right now. She began limping her way south, following the river, her eyes scanning the base of the cliff for a safe place to hide. She walked and limped, stumbling often, exhaustion pulling at her tired body. She was so tired she was crying, and she knew her tears were leaving streaks on her dirty face. She nearly yelled for joy when she spotted a small overhang of rock. She turned and made her way to her temporary haven.

* * * *

"Where is she, you motherfucker?" Sam yelled into the Chief of Police's face, shaking him by the hold he had on the man's shirtfront.

"I don't know. She knocked me out and took off."

"You cowardly piece of shit. You and your brother-in-law are going down. An officer in Miami has all the evidence needed to send you and your colleagues away for the rest of your life. If I didn't know you'd be dead soon, I'd kill you myself."

"Sam, let him go," Damon said calmly. Sam felt Damon place his hand on his shoulder, trying to restrain him. "Hand him over to the Feds. We need to find Rachel before it gets dark."

The place was swarming with the law. Luke's friends he affectionately called the Delaney Shadows, Daniel and Britt, as well as Seamus, Connell, Luke, Damon, Tyson, Sam, and the FBI, were all combing the area, looking for clues as to where Rachel was headed.

Sam shoved Rachel's ex-boss so hard the bastard fell on his ass. He turned away, not once looking back at the piece of scum, and headed outside. They needed to find Rachel. God only knew what state she was going to be in. The bastard said he hadn't hurt her, only tied her up, but he could be lying. Sam had never felt so out of control before. He was usually an emotionless hard-ass, working his way through a mission with taciturn, calculating determination. The fact it was their woman, the love of his life, missing had a large knot of fear eating away at his insides. He had to get himself under control. He breathed in deeply, held the breath for three seconds, and slowly released it. He repeated the calming process over and over until the knot in his gut began to recede. He looked up at his brothers' hard faces and knew he had the same look on his face. They had a job to do, and emotion was the last thing they needed crowding their minds and their judgment. They needed to be detached, hard-ass warriors.

The Osborn brothers, with Sheriff Luke Sun-Walker and the Delaney brothers, got to work, searching the area with a fine-tooth comb. A yell from Daniel Delaney had Sam and everyone else rushing over to where he stood studying the ground behind the small cabin.

"She headed west. Let's go," Daniel's deep, rough voice commanded.

Sam and the others walked for hours, their direction changing as signs of flight caught their eyes. They reached a deep ravine, and Sam searched down the sheer cliff face, praying their woman wasn't at the bottom.

"Over here," Luke yelled. He pointed to the disturbed ground, a scuff mark from a shoe and a broken tree branch indicating which way to go.

They made it to the place Rachel had gone over the edge of the cliff just as twilight set in. They were going to have to wait until daylight before they went any further. As much as Sam wanted to keep going, his training kicked in, knowing he would endanger his own life and the lives of the men with him if they tried to keep going.

Daniel and Britt Delaney got a fire going and handed around energy bars and water canteens they'd pulled from their backpacks to all the men. The brothers were veritable Boy Scouts, having everything needed for a night out under the stars. The eight men relaxed around the fire, some dozing, the others conversing as they whiled away the hours until dawn.

Sam saw Daniel pull his portable tracker from the clip on his hip, and wondered why he looked annoyed.

"What's wrong?" Sam asked.

"My tracking device still isn't working."

"Hey, Daniel, where did you get that thing?" Luke asked from across the fire.

"Standard issue."

"Shit, man, what the hell are you and your brother into?" Tyson asked.

"Classified," Britt answered.

Sam sighed as the conversation died down with the fire. Most of the men looked totally relaxed, but looks were deceiving. The slightest out-of-place sound would have him and the others all drawing their weapons. They were all warriors, some more elite than others, but they all lived to protect the innocent. It's what he and the rest of the group had been trained for.

* * * *

Rachel shifted on the hard rock beneath her tired, aching body for what felt like the hundredth time. She was so tired and hungry, but she was alive. Her right ankle hurt so badly now that the adrenaline had worn off, and she was on the verge of tears. She felt sick to her stomach with the knowledge she wouldn't be able to continue on. She either had a very bad sprain or she'd fractured a bone in her ankle. It was almost three times its normal size, black and blue all around her ankle. Her feet hurt from all the cuts and scrapes, and they felt like they were on fire. It felt as if they were scraped raw, no skin left to protect her soles. She dozed on and off, every little rustle and sound bringing her alert to listen for danger. She was shaking with cold, but knew it was more in reaction to her situation than the ambient temperature. She wished she had had the foresight to keep her cell phone in her pocket instead of her purse. Hindsight was a wonderful thing, after the fact. There probably wasn't any reception out here anyway. Rachel finally drifted down into a deep slumber, emotional and physical exhaustion catching up with her. She dreamed of her men, safe and sound, out looking for her.

* * * *

"Okay, let's head out," Damon stated, eager to find their woman. The sun hadn't risen completely yet, but there was enough light for the men to work and move by. Sam was the first over the cliff. Damon watched as his brother moved with stealthy grace, his muscles rippling as he moved steadily down the cliff side.

"She made it safely to the ground," Sam called up to the other men when his feet touched flat, firmer ground. "I'll scout her direction."

Damon watched as Sam followed Rachel's track and found where she'd stopped to drink. Damon praised her in his mind. He followed as Sam tracked her path silently, steadily. Pride filled his chest at what their woman had endured. She was a lot tougher than he or his brothers thought. The instinct for survival had kicked in, and he knew she wouldn't relent until she was safe and sound back in their arms.

Damon and the others traveled for another couple of miles, all eyes scanning the ground, the river, the base of the cliff. They walked silently, their military training natural and instinctive. Daniel was in the lead now. He'd been moving quietly but quickly. Then Damon saw him stop, tilting his head as he held his hand up for silence. Damon and the other men behind him froze, watching the huge man until he indicated all was right again. He saw Daniel take one step, stop, turn, and face him and his brothers.

"Your woman is asleep under the overhang, twenty meters away at two o'clock," Daniel called, and the Osborn brothers took off, weapons drawn, eyes scanning.

The sight of a dirty, disheveled female curled in the fetal position, fast asleep on a large rock, was the most beautiful sight Damon had ever seen. They replaced their weapons, out of sight from Rachel, and walked over to where she slept. She didn't move or look like she was going to wake anytime soon.

Damon, Sam, and Tyson knelt down at her side, placed their hands on her warm body, and gently began to stroke her awake. She sat up screaming as she blinked her eyes back into focus, her gaze going from one brother to the next, then back again. She surprised Damon when she jumped up and grabbed hold of all three of them and didn't let go.

She was safe. They had found her. Damon felt the knot of fear in his gut finally leave now that she was back in his arms once more.

Chapter Fourteen

Rachel lay beneath the arbor roof, lazing the hours away in the hammock her men had bought for her, her healing foot propped up on a cushion. The book she had been reading lay pages down on her stomach. Her eyes closed as she relished the peace and quiet of the late-spring afternoon. It had been just over a week since her men had found her. Her ex-boss and his brother-in-law were incarcerated, the chance of release nonexistent. The female hit woman had disappeared from the face of the Earth.

Rachel's mom was now back home, her bodyguard now living with her, as her boyfriend. It was strange how life's circumstances and coincidences twisted and turned. She pondered whether it was fate, or if they all had guardian angels looking out for them, directing them all to where they should be.

The only thing that would make Rachel happier would be to have her men truly back in her bed. She hadn't slept alone since she'd come back home, but none of her men had touched her sexually. She was becoming a bundle of sexually frustrated nerves. She wanted to strip her men bare-ass naked and ravish them until none of them could stand. They were treating her like a piece of fragile crystal. Hadn't she proven to them she wasn't as frail as she looked?

Rachel had been given the all clear to return to work on Monday and hoped the normality of reality would show her men she was more than ready to take them on. The sound of three cars pulling up in the driveway drew her head around. The slam of the front door, followed by three sets of male footsteps, was like music to her ears. Her men weren't supposed to be home just yet, so she wondered what was going on.

"Rachel?" Sam's anxious voice drifted through the open dining room doors.

"Out here," she called back.

The sight of her three men shoving each other, trying to be the first out the door, was comical. They looked like little boys fighting over a toy.

"What's up?" Rachel asked.

"We are, baby," Damon replied.

It took her a moment, but when the penny dropped, she burst out laughing. She glanced down at their crotches, her breath hitching when she saw their huge erections pushing against the zippers of their pants.

"How come you're all home? I thought it would be at least another hour or so before you were here. Tyson, you've only been gone a few hours. Who's looking after the pub?"

"Connell and Seamus are. They've decided they're working for me until they figure out what they want to do with regards to their careers. I have the rest of the afternoon and night off, sugar," Tyson explained, a wicked smile on his face as he waggled his eyebrows at her.

"Hm, that's good. So, what are you going to do? I can see some weeds peeking through the ground that need to be pulled," Rachel teased. She watched a pained expression cross her men's faces and pouts form on their lips. She couldn't contain her mirth. She practically doubled over as she burst into laughter. The laughing changed to a squawk when large, gentle, but firm hands scooped her up from the hammock and tossed her over a broad, muscular shoulder.

"Think you're funny, don't ya, sugar?" Tyson said, patting her ass with a light slap.

"We'll see who has the last laugh, big boy," Rachel goaded saucily.

Rachel reached down and grabbed a handful of firm, muscular

buttock, eliciting a growl of approval from Tyson. She bounced on his shoulder as he rushed into the house, heading straight for her room. She lifted her head, peering through her hair, smiling at Sam and Damon as they followed close behind.

Rachel's world spun, her eyes blurring, and then she was bouncing on the mattress in her room. The sexual, predatory looks her three men gave her made her heartbeat speed up, her breath panting in and out of her lungs and her pussy softening and weeping with arousal. They moved as one, hands reaching, tugging, and pulling until she was totally naked before them, spread out like a sacrifice on an altar. She watched as their hands began discarding their own clothes, practically ripping them from their bodies with eagerness. Her eyes roved the breadth and length of their bodies, her breath catching at the beauty the three men revealed to her. They were all so drop-dead gorgeous, brawny and way too sexy. Their muscles rippled as they moved, drawing her eyes to biceps, pecs, abs, and quads and everything in between. They were sex personified, oozing confidence, which only heightened her awareness and arousal.

Rachel stared as the three men closed the gap between them and her. She had waited far too long for this day. The last eight days had been the longest of her life. She was grabbing hold with both hands, not willing to let go, and not willing to look back.

Rachel watched as Tyson crawled on the bed near her feet. On his hands and knees, he nudged her legs apart, his big body moving closer to her. She locked gazes with him, but was still very aware of Damon and Sam climbing on the bed on either side of her. Tyson knelt between her splayed thighs, rubbing his hands up and down the inside of her legs. He reached for her hips, held them between his hands, and tilted her pelvis up. He kept eye contact with her, lowered his head until he was inches away from her pussy, and inhaled deeply.

"God, you smell good, sugar. But I bet you taste even better," Tyson stated as he lowered his head.

The first touch of Tyson's tongue on Rachel's clit was so decadent and pleasurable she lifted her hips up into his mouth. She would never be able to get her fill of her three men. She was going to spend the rest of her life loving them, physically as well as emotionally. She reached down, threaded her fingers through his hair, and gave herself over to her lovers. Tyson worked at Rachel's cunt, giving her pleasure beyond her imagination.

Sam gently directed her face to him, the palm of his hand on her cheek. She sobbed out her pleasure as Tyson thrust two fingers into her tight, wet hole, her eyes on Sam's as he leaned forward, placing his lips on hers. His kiss was so gentle and full of love, but still so carnal she couldn't catch her breath. Then Damon's hand and mouth were on her breasts. She was in heaven and hell. Heaven to be back in the arms of her lovers once more, and hell because she wanted her men to fuck her, right *now*. Rachel mewled out her frustration when Tyson withdrew his mouth and fingers from her pussy. Sam withdrew his mouth from hers, and Damon removed his mouth and hand from her breasts.

"Easy, sugar. We'll give you what you need," Tyson crooned. He picked her up, moved to the head of the bed, and leaned against the pillows cushioning his back. He pulled her up and over his hips so she was straddling him as they faced each other. "Take me into your sexy, wet pussy, Rach. I want you to ride me, sugar."

They kept eye contact as Rachel kneeled up, aligning her pussy with Tyson's cock. She slowly lowered herself onto his hard dick, the mushroom-shaped head separating her wet folds, easing into her cunt as she slowly lowered herself. They both groaned as Tyson embedded his cock in her cunt and she enveloped him. Rachel rocked up and down, easing Tyson's cock into her wet sheath with every move. The feel of Tyson grabbing her hips and pulling her down, impaling her on his hard cock, sent her over the edge. She threw her head back and screamed, her pussy grabbing and releasing around Tyson's hard rod.

"I love watching and feeling you come on my cock, sugar. I love you, Rachel." Tyson breathed against her sensitive ear.

"I love you, too, Tyson. I love all of you so much." Rachel sobbed, her heart full to overflowing.

"Ah, baby, I love you, too. I'm about to show you how much," Damon said before he placed a cold, wet finger at the pucker of Rachel's anus. He massaged the lube into the skin of her ass. She felt her tight muscles relax, and she heard him get more lube as he pushed two fingers into her ass. She moaned as he pumped his fingers in and out, slow and steady, letting her body adjust to the intrusion. When she was totally relaxed, he withdrew his fingers, covered the latex on his cock with lube, and began to work his way into her ass. The sound of his groan as his balls met the flesh of her cunt, his cock throbbing in time to her own heartbeat, had her internal muscles fluttering and rippling around his cock. She turned her head when Sam reached over, placing the palm of his hand on her cheek. Sam ran the head of his cock over her blood-swollen lips, and she flicked her tongue out, twirling it around the top of his dick, and smiled at the three low, masculine groans. It was the catalyst that broke her men's leashed control.

Damon pulled out of Rachel's ass, making her moan with pleasure. As he pushed back in, Tyson slid his cock out of Rachel's pussy, and she sucked Sam's cock into her mouth to the back of her throat. Her men increased the pace slowly, and she was glad, as she didn't want to end such bliss too soon, but knew she would be unable to stop the inevitable conclusion. The sensation of her Kegel muscles rippling along Tyson's and Damon's cocks must have been too much for her lovers to bear. They both drew back at the same time and slammed their hips back into her. The sound of flesh slapping flesh, and her own mouth making slurping sounds as she sucked Sam's cock, echoed throughout the room. She was beyond control and knew by the frantic pumping of her lovers' hips and their moans of pleasure that they were also beyond control.

Rachel was in nirvana. The sensation of her men loving her at the same time was pure bliss. The slide and glide of her men's cocks thrusting in and out of her body was nearly more than she could stand. She never wanted to stop. She squeezed her internal muscles, gripping Tyson's and Damon's cocks as she sucked hard on Sam. The groans her actions elicited from her men made her feel so feminine and powerful. She seemed to have unleashed the inner-animal instincts of her men. The pace of their loving changed from steady, countering thrusts to fast, hard, and deep. She couldn't get enough. The aesthetics of their cocks plunging in and out of her pussy and ass at the same time was making her fly up the mountain side at a rapid pace. Her pelvic floor muscles fluttered and quivered, gathering into a tight coil, ready to snap and spring open, hurtling her to the top. She was about to come undone, and in a big way. She wasn't scared of the sensation. She faced it head-on, willing it to come get her. Her body froze, her muscles tight as she hovered on the precipice of the mountain. Then she was flung up and out, stars hovering before her eyes, but she was more aware of her men than ever before.

Rachel heard Sam shout, his cock pulsing and spurting his cum to the back of her throat. She gulped frantically, swallowing down every drop of his essence, released him with an audible pop, threw her head up, and screamed her release. She heard Damon and Tyson roaring out their own climaxes and was happy they all fell over the edge into bliss together. When the last ripple and shudder finally ebbed to a stop, the four of them slumped down onto the bed to catch their breath.

Rachel groaned when Damon pulled his semiflaccid cock from her ass, but sighed as Tyson rolled with her, lying beside her on the mattress. His semihard cock slipped out of her pussy, but she was too satiated to move to the bathroom to clean up. Her eyes were closed, her eyelids too heavy to keep open, but she knew the smile on her face said everything. She fell into a light doze until one of her men began to clean her up with a warm, wet cloth. She opened her eye to a slit, giving Sam a return smile, then closed her eye again. Rachel had never been happier. She was surrounded by her men, their bodies touching hers, their warmth offering comfort and love.

"Rachel, are you awake, baby?" Damon asked quietly from beside her.

"Uh-huh."

"Let us help you sit up, darlin', we have a surprise for you," Sam said, reaching beneath her arms and helping her to lean against the pillows resting on the headboard.

Rachel's heavy eyelids lifted so she could look at her men. They all had smiles on their faces that would give the Cheshire cat a run for its money. She watched as Tyson and Sam hurried from the bedroom. She heard a pop, then a curse, and couldn't help but giggle. She knew what that sound was. She wondered if Sam had aimed the cork at Tyson on purpose. The clatter of dishes, the clink of glasses, and the sound of their returning footsteps made her turn to watch the doorway. They appeared moments later with a tray adorned with a platter of fruit, cheese, and crackers, with four glasses off to the side. Rachel pulled her legs up, giving Sam and Tyson room. They crawled onto the bed carefully, bringing the tray with them. Sam handed out the champagne glasses, while Tyson set the platter on the bed in the middle of the four of them.

"What are we celebrating?" Rachel asked as she took the proffered glass in hand.

"You. Us. Love," Damon said.

"You guys are so sweet," Rachel replied, tears in her eyes. "I love you all, so much. You've given me back my life. I didn't think I would live long enough to follow my dreams and heart."

"What is your heart's desire, sugar?" Tyson asked unexpectedly.

Rachel looked into each of her lovers' eyes, stopping on them in turn, and spoke from her heart.

"You are, Tyson. You also, Sam. And you as well, Damon. You are all so special. I love you more than I could ever express with words. I would like nothing better than to spend the rest of my life loving you all," Rachel stated honestly. Now that she had the chance of a future, she wasn't about to waste it being afraid.

"Drink your champagne, baby," Damon said quietly.

Rachel felt a huge lump forming in her chest. She'd hoped to get some sort of response from her men. They'd already told her they loved her. So, what was going on? She lowered her eyes to her glass, something in the bottom attracting her attention. She squinted her eyes and stared until she felt as if she was going cross eyed. She blinked and looked again. Yep, it was still there, so it wasn't her imagination. Rachel put the glass to her lips and drank deeply. She didn't stop until the ring slid into her mouth. She placed two fingers against her lips and pulled it out to inspect it. It was the most beautiful ring she had ever seen. Three strands of white gold entwined into a Celtic knot, and a lone blue sapphire took center stage in the middle. Rachel lifted her eyes to see three hot, sexy guys smiling at her, the love they had for her shining from their eyes.

"We love you so much, darlin'. Will you marry us? Spend the rest of your life with us? Have babies with us and grow old with us?" Sam asked.

Rachel looked deeply into each of her lovers' eyes, smiled, and simply answered, "Yes."

They took turns feeding her, lavishing her with love and attention. She'd never known a person could get creative with food. Her three lovers taught her a whole lot throughout the rest of the afternoon and long into the night. She couldn't wait to start the rest of her life with her men. She had no idea how things worked in a ménage relationship, and even though she cared deeply for her men and they for her, she didn't really worry about the schematics of their union. She would marry whomever they chose for her to marry, but she would be a wife to all three of them, in her heart, for as long as she lived.

Rachel gave herself up to her men as they loved her body. They sent her to the stars over and over again throughout the night, but she made damn sure they were with her every step of the way. She had six months of her life to make up for, and she was going to spend every spare minute she had loving her men.

"Rachel, do you care who you marry on paper?" Sam asked from her side, his quiet voice a whisper in the dark of the night.

"No, Sam. As long as I am with all of you, for the rest of our lives, I don't care what a piece of paper says. To me, you are all my husbands from this night on."

"I love you, darlin'. You're perfect for us," Sam said.

"I love you, too, Sam. You and your brothers were sent to me from the angels," Rachel whispered. Her eyes closed once more. They were too heavy to keep open. She drifted to sleep, snuggled up to and surrounded by her three husbands, keeping her warm, safe, and making her feel loved.

She was one lucky woman.

THE END

WWW.BECCAVAN-EROTICROMANCE.COM

ABOUT THE AUTHOR

My name is Becca Van. I live in Australia with my wonderful hubby of many years, as well as my children, a pigeon pair (a girl and a boy). I have always wanted to write and last year decided to do just that.

I didn't want to stay in the mainstream of a boring nine-to-five job, so I quit, fulfilling my passion for writing. I decided to utilize my time with something I knew I would enjoy and had always wanted to do. I submitted my first manuscript to Siren-BookStrand a couple of months ago, and much to my excited delight, I got a reply saying they would love to publish my story. I literally jump out of bed with excitement each day and can't wait for my laptop to power up so I can get to work.

Also by Becca Van

Ménage Everlasting: Slick Rock 1: *Slick Rock Cowboys*
Ménage Everlasting: Slick Rock 2: *Double E Ranch*
Ménage Everlasting: Slick Rock 4: *Leah's Irish Heroes*
Ménage Everlasting: Slick Rock 5: *Her Shadow Men*
Ménage Everlasting: Slick Rock 6: *Her Personal Security*

For all other titles, please visit
www.bookstrand.com/becca-van

Siren Publishing, Inc.
www.SirenPublishing.com

CPSIA information can be obtained at www.ICGtesting.com
Printed in the USA
BVOW03s0752281114

377069BV00035B/1079/P